THE GAYEST CHRISTMAS PAGEANT EVER!

A COMEDY IN TWO ACTS

BY JOE MARSHALL

THE GAYEST CHRISTMAS PAGEANT EVER!
© 2007-2019 Joe Marshall. All rights reserved.

ISBN 978-1-79473-664-1

SPECIAL NOTE

SPECIAL NOTE ON SONGS AND RECORDINGS

THE GAYEST CHRISTMAS PAGEANT EVER!, the original Off-Broadway production, was presented by Adrian Maynard and Joe Marshall in association with Alternative Theatre Company, Inc. at The Actors' Playhouse in New York City on November 13, 2009, and closed on January 3, 2010. It was directed by Joe Marshall; the scenery was by Duane Pagano; the costumes were by Rachel Dozier-Ezell; the lighting was by Duane Pagano; the sound design was by Joe Marshall; the assistant director was Arlonda Washington; and the production stage manager was Jenny Waletzky. The cast, in order of appearance, was as follows:

FEMALE REPORTER . . . . Rachel Wright
ROD . . . . Jason B. Schmidt
MANNY . . . . Adam Weinstock
JIM . . . . .Ryan Wright
DON . . . . Blaine Pennington
TARQUIN . . . . .Jonathan Chang
SAM, KING HEROD, HANDSOME MAN, PROTESTOR . . . . .Ben Jones
M&M, SHEPHERD ONE, PROTESTOR . . . . Chris von Hoffman
MONICA, PROTESTOR . . . . Emily Schramel
JESUS, PROTESTOR . . . . Alvaro Sena
MARGIE . . . . Crystal V. Cotton
JANET . . . . .Elyse Beyer
MARTHA . . . . .Ree Davis
ACTOR ONE, WISE MAN THREE . . . . Jamey Nicholas
TINA, MARY, PROTESTOR . . . . .Heather Shields
SPIKE, JOSEPH . . . . Bryan Zoppi
TYRONE . . . . .Kershel Anthony
ACTOR THREE, SANTA CLAUS PUPPET, WISE MAN ONE, PROTESTOR . . . . .James Stewart
TED . . . . Evan Schultz
SHEPHERD TWO . . . . John Paul Venuti
TYRONE'S MOTHER, PROTESTOR . . . . .Kymberlie Joseph
INNKEEPER, WISE MAN TWO, TYRONE'S FATHER . . . . Dorian McGhee
ALEX, PROTESTOR . . . . Alexandra Dickson

THE GAYEST CHRISTMAS PAGEANT EVER! was originally produced by Alternative Theatre Company, Inc. at the Temple of Music and Art, Tucson, Arizona, December, 2008.

ORIGINAL OFF-BROADWAY PRODUCTION PHOTOS (2009)

NOTES FROM THE PLAYWRIGHT

"The moment comedy technique becomes obvious to the audience, the humor is lost."
-John E. Dietrich

"We must never get caught trying to be funny."
- William Ball

Note to Actors
In all of my work, the actor should avoid playing for laughs. Always be in the moment and play the situation. The humor must not appear to be forced. It must appear to naturally spring from the humor of the situation. If you get a laugh on a line, do not punch the line harder the next performance. Sometimes an actor will get a laugh on a line and then decide to overplay it the next time out. This rarely works.

About the Craigslist monologue
This was an actual monologue that's been sent around the Internet and went viral. I'm not sure if it's really a Craigslist posting or an email prank, but it worked for the show. The actual idea came from a Podcast on acting I was frequently listening to when I first moved to New York. In response to a question from an actor looking for an original monologue, the host suggesting looking at postings on Craigslist. For some reason I found it humorous. So I took the Craigslist viral monologue and simply tweaked it a little. In performance it brought the house down every night! Who knew it would be so popular.

Note to Directors
My work has a very fast paced rhythm. If you find it, the laughs come naturally. Moments are never made to "play the joke."

Alex/Angel should look, talk and act very butch. When she plays the Angel think of the voice of Glinda the good witch.

The role of Ted can be played several ways. For the original Off-Broadway production we had both sexes playing Ted. (Our swing was a female.) So let the actors create the character. We've had the lisping Ted as described in the script, and the swing actress played the role as a Valley Girl who channeled an evangelical preacher in the Pageant scene.

The flash back parents scene in Act Two can be played very simply by having actors wear pieces of clothing (i.e. wigs, hats, scarves, etc.) that suggest the time period.

The Takes to the audience in the pageant scene are just that. They are fast, and are best when accented with a quick light change.

For the voiceover of Jesus in Act Two, Jim is the only person who can hear Jesus' voice. All other actors are replying to Rod's information on being "Sold Out." Jim thinks they heard Jesus. They all think Jim is talking about Rod's comment.

Have fun with this show. We sure did!

All my best,

Joe Marshall

TIME

The present. Mid-November.

PLACE

West Hollywood, California.

SETTING

All the action takes place on an empty stage at the Triangle Theatre Company, a small LGBTQ theatre in West Hollywood, California. It is time for their annual Christmas pageant.

CHARACTERS

Female Reporter / Tina / Mary – attractive, late 20's or early 30's
Rod / Monica / King Herod – male, late 40's
Manny – male, mid-50's
Jim – male, late 20's
Don – male, early 30's
Tarquin – male, mid-20's, effeminate
Sam / Shepherd Two / Gerald – male, 20's
M&M / Shepherd One / Steve – male, 20's
Jesus – male, Hispanic
Margie / Tyrone's Father – female, late 30's or early 40's, African American
Janet – female, 20's
Martha – female, 90's
Actor One / Actor Three / Wise Man One / Wise Man Three / Santa Puppet – male
Spike / Joseph – male, effeminate
Tyrone – male, 30's, African American
Alex / Angel – female, masculine
Ted – male
Innkeeper / Wise Man Two / Tyrone's Mother – male, African American
Handsome Man – male, attractive, 20's

Any available actor may play protestors in the first scene.

SCENES

ACT 1

Scene 1 – A Dance Studio Before the Date
Scene 2 – Stan's Apartment After the Date
Scene 3 – Empty Stage, One Hour Later
Scene 4 – Meet the Director
Scene 5 – Auditions

ACT 2

Scene 1 – The Rehearsal
Scene 2 – Stage, Alley, Past, Present
Scene 3 – Opening Night Jitters
Scene 4 – The Pageant
Scene 5 – The Morning After
Scene 6 – Sidewalk In Front of Triangle Theatre

ACT 1
SCENE 1

The sidewalk in front of The Triangle Theatre Company. As house lights fade loud chanting is heard. At rise a group of protestors is seen holding signs that read "No show," "Gays must go," and "Sacrilege!" and "Jesus Hates Flags." One male dressed in back wears a red MAGA hat. A female reporter from FOX NEWS enters…

FEMALE REPORTER: Yes, good evening Tucker, I'm standing outside the Triangle Theatre Company in the heart of West Hollywood, a city well known for its nightlife, celebrity culture, and diverse atmosphere. But for the past two months protesters and missionaries alike have descended upon this small nonprofit LGBTQ theatre. Rumors have surfaced that Jesus Christ has returned, and has chosen, of all places, this small community theatre. If that's not unbelievable enough, there are claims of miracles, the burning of the baby Jesus, even gender changing, and all of it centers around a small Christmas pageant, a pageant that received horrible reviews, "The Gayest Christmas Pageant Ever," which has been completely sold out for the last four weeks and shows no signs of slowing down. *(A few actors enter stage left, disguised under large hats and sunglasses.)*

FEMALE REPORTER: It looks as if the actors have arrived. Maybe we can get one of them to answer some questions. *(To the group of actors.)* Hello, may we ask you a few Questions?

ONE ACTOR: *(grabbing her microphone)* Baba booey, Howard Stern!

(She takes her microphone back as he and all actors rush past the crowd and into the theatre. Rod, an older, well-dressed male in his late thirties or early forties enters, followed by Manny, a very distinguished looking older Hispanic man in his mid thirties or forties.)

FEMALE REPORTER: *(To Rod.)* Are you involved with this production?

ROD: Involved? I wrote it! *(Protesters boo)*

MAGA GUY: Trump 2020!

ROD: Oh hell no, who said that?

FEMALE REPORTER: *(To Manny.)* And you sir?

MANNY: I'm his partner.

ROD: And one of the producers.

FEMALE REPORTER: Could you enlighten us about the rumors involving this production?

ROD: What rumors?

FEMALE REPORTER: The burning of the baby Jesus?

ROD: Oh please, all lies, I'll tell you what happened. *(takes microphone)* Hi Shepard, love ya girl! Well, it all started when Jim, the straight technical director, purchased a gay slang handbook. You see, we were a few hours away from our Christmas Pageant production meeting… *(The protestors separate, revealing Jim, a young man in his late twenties, dressed in jeans, work belt and t-shirt splattered with multi-colored old paint, sitting on a bar stool. Next to him is a second chair and a ghost light. He holds a rolled joint in one hand and reads from a small hand book.)*

JIM: *(Reading the cover.)* "Gay Slang." *(Opens and start to read quickly.)* Congratulations, Heterosexual Male, on your purchase of this book. By doing so you have embarked upon the first step in educating yourself about the gay community. Chapter one: learning gay slang. Gay slang, or LGBT slang in linguistics, refers to a form of English slang used predominantly by the gay, lesbian, bisexual and transgender community. It's mandatory to learn their terminology in order to prevent you, the heterosexual male, from getting lost in a conversation, as detailed in the table below: Glossary of gay slang taken from Polari. Word: Chicken. Approximate meaning: Young boy. Word: Girl. Approximate meaning: Young boy or older man. Phrase: Oh no you di-uhhnt! Approximate meaning: Oh, no you did not. This phrase is emphasized with a head shake and one finger in the air. See example A-1 below. *(Follows example putting one finger in the air and shaking his head.)* Oh no you di-uhhnt!

ROD: *(From off stage.)* Hello?

JIM: Oh no, party's over! *(Jim closes the book, turns off ghost light, and exits as Rod enters carrying a few large shopping bags.)*

ROD: *(Loudly.)* A little light please! *(No response.)* Do I have to do everything around here? *(Rod attempts to turn on the ghost light. It sparks, he screams.)* Holy Mary Mother of God! Jim! *(The ghost light turns on.)* What the hell! *(Jim enters and stands behind Rod who hasn't noticed him.)* Jim!

JIM: *(Calmly.)* Yes?

ROD: *(Startled.)* Jesus! *(Composed, he starts to pick up the bags.)* Please, Jim, fix this ghost light before someone electrocutes himself! Really, auditions are three weeks away.

JIM: Consider it done. What's in the bags?

ROD: I already started buying props, and last minute Christmas gifts. *(Calling out.)* Manny! Where the hell… Manny! *(Jim exits.)*

MANNY: *(Off stage.)* I'm coming.

ROD: *(Talking to Jim.)* I think he ignores me on purpose. *(He turns to find Jim gone.)* Now where the hell did *he* go? *(Stage lights snap on.)*

ROD: Finally. *(Manny enters.)*

MANNY: I was trying to get the new lighting board unpacked. *(Rod holds out two shopping bags as Manny takes them.)*

ROD: Don't peek into those boxes, they're Christmas gifts. What the hell is that smell?

MANNY: Take a guess.

ROD: Jim?

MANNY: *Smells* like Jim.

ROD: I told him no pot, marijuana, smoking in this theater. JIM! I told you we shouldn't hire an STD.

MANNY: A what?

ROD: Straight Technical Director. *(Manny looks in the bags.)*

MANNY: What's all this?

ROD: Props for the Christmas pageant. *(Manny looks in the bags again.)* It was cheap!

MANNY: How much?

ROD: Three hundred.

MANNY: Three?!

ROD: We can splurge; the Christmas Pageant brings in a shit load of money.

MANNY: That shit load of money pulls us out of the red.

ROD: See; thank God for Jesus and faggots.

MANNY: It helps us cover the cost of your other flops.

ROD: I do *not* produce flops!

MANNY: What about "Okla-Homo?"

ROD: That was a summer stock show!

MANNY: In March?

ROD: It was clever!

MANNY: It was a lawsuit threat and an immediate cease and desist certified letter from the lawyers representing the Rogers and Hammerstein estate.

ROD: Those petty people. One show!

MANNY: What about your gay version of "The Wizard of OZ?"

ROD: A masterpiece!

MANNY: A bad title.

ROD: There was nothing wrong with the title!

MANNY: "The Wizard Is *Odd*."

ROD: You didn't understand the premise.

MANNY: The premise? *(Rod starts to unpack some of the gifts and props.)* You changed Dorothy into a Mormon boy named Timothy who was swept away by a tornado from Provo, Utah, and dropped into the heart of the San Francisco Castro district, where he meets a leather daddy, a lesbian and a drag queen…

ROD: *(Correcting him.)* Female *illusionist*.

MANNY: The wizard was straight in a land of all gay people, making him the odd man out, which is what I believe enticed you to title the play "The Wizard is Odd," and it flopped.

ROD: Two shows, big deal.

MANNY: Then there was your musical about the miniature golf course on Coney Island.

ROD: "Glory Holes of Coney Island," a fabulous title!

MANNY: A flop.

ROD: Oh! I almost forgot! Ta da! *(Rod presents a Christmas tree topper.)*

MANNY: What is that?

ROD: It's the tree topper for our Christmas Pageant this year.

MANNY: Another Santa, Rod? We have over thirty of them!

ROD: No, not like this.

MANNY: Why, is he gay?

ROD: No! It's the snow-shitting Santa!

MANNY: You're shitting me.

ROD: No, check this out. *(Showing him the box.)* The snow shoots out of his butt! Cute.

MANNY: *(Pauses, stares at Rod.)* You've lost it.

ROD: What's wrong with it?

MANNY: Well, ignoring the fact that it's crude, your Mother.

ROD: She'll love it.

MANNY: My Mother?

ROD: She'll deal.

MANNY: Jim's Mother?

ROD: She is *not* going to be here!

MANNY: Oh, but she is.

ROD: No! The woman has Tourette's and is a narcoleptic. When she's not asleep, she's awake yelling out obscenities.

MANNY: You stress way too much. She's not going to be here, it was a "what-if."

ROD: You instigate. Regardless, it's a Christmas Pageant, *our* Christmas Pageant, *our* theatre, *our* tree, *our* Santa.

MANNY: Shitting all over it!

ROD: It's not shit, it's snow. Fake snow.

MANNY: Rod, we really need to talk about…

DON: *(From off stage right.)* Hello? Anyone here?

MANNY: *(Yelling to Don.)* On stage Don.

ROD: Let's get another opinion. If Don hates the idea, I'll concede by not putting it on the tree. However, if in fact he likes it, *on* the tree it goes. Deal?

MANNY: Deal. *(Don enters. He's a handsome man in his early thirties. throughout the scene he's checking messages and texting on his cellphone.)*

DON: Hey guys.

MANNY: Hey Don.

DON: Tarquin here yet?

MANNY: I haven't seen him.

ROD: *(Overly nice.)* Hello Don. How are you?

DON: Doing good. *(texting)*

ROD: Nice.

DON: A little tired.

ROD: Would you like some coffee?

MANNY: Ask him.

ROD: I will.

DON: Ask me what?

MANNY: Here, let me show you… *(Manny takes tree topper box from Rod and tries to show it to Don. Rod grabs the box back from Manny.)*

ROD: It's my Santa, I'll show him. *(Rod hides the box behind his back.)* Don, you have an open mind, right?

MANNY: Rod bought a scatting Santa.

ROD: Manny!

DON: *(first time he actually is looking up from his phone)* A what?

MANNY: A Santa that shits snow, Rod's sick idea of a tree topper.

ROD: *(Holding out Santa.)* He poops snow. *(Laughs.)* Funny huh? See, he shits snow.

DON: Yeah, I see… It's funny. *(back to texting)*

ROD: *(Victory.)* Yes!

MANNY: Don, *(taking Don's phone)* you would not object to that… thing… being on the top of our pageant Christmas tree!

DON: What? I thought you bought this for your own *personal* tree.

RON: No. That would be a waste. *(To Manny.)* Don said it was funny. I win! I'm going to try it out. *(Rod exits.)*

MANNY: *(handing his phone back)* Thanks for saying it's funny.

DON: It is funny, just not center stage funny. *(texting)* You sure the new guy will go for that?

MANNY: I doubt it. Oh, and speaking of that, Rod has no clue.

DON: You didn't tell him yet? Manny, the new playwright is going to be here in an hour or less.

MANNY: What! Why?

DON: *(Placing cell phone in his pocket)* To meet Tarquin, the costumer, *(sarcastically)* and, oh, I don't know Manny, maybe because he's directing *his* Christmas play on *our* stage. Why did *you* wait this long to tell Rod?

MANNY: Because Rod's not exactly the easiest person to talk to.

DON: Manny, let's be honest, whatever Rod writes, directs, touches, flops.

MANNY: Thanks.

DON: Excluding you. Manny, listen to me, this is our opportunity to produce a new exciting Christmas pageant. This playwright is a genius, and he'll be here in less than an hour to talk about casting what I believe will be our best pageant ever. Manny, I hate reminding you, but I can't continually invest my own personal finances into another year of bad productions.

MANNY: I know, I hear you, it's appreciated, all your patience and support, but Rod believes it's his Christmas pageant that brings in the money, not you. I even told him there were no comps.

DON: They were *all* complimentary tickets.

MANNY: That's not true, some people paid… *(They look at each other)* some… a few…

DON: Five! How long are you going to be playing this game? *(Tarquin enters. He is a young eccentric costume designer carrying several bolts of fabric.)*

DON: Tarquin.

TARQUIN: Read the new Christmas play...sooooo much better than the shit Rod writes. *(Rod enters with two manuscripts in hand.)*

ROD: Tarquin.

TARQUIN: *(as if saying hello)* Psycho bitch from hell. *(To Manny, referring to Rod.)* She know yet?

MANNY: He will.

DON: Now?

MANNY: Now.

DON: Good.

TARQUIN: *(To Rod)* All the world's a stage, a flat stage where some bitches fall off the edges. *(exits)*

ROD: What was that about?

MANNY: Nothing. *(Don gives Manny a look.)* Well, something. We need to talk.

ROD: Ok, but not right now... Look at this. *(Handing Manny the script.)*

MANNY: What is it?

ROD: *(Proudly.)* My new Christmas script.

MANNY: Good. Rod...

ROD: Took me a whole week to write.

DON: A week?

ROD: Yes, a week, can you believe it?

MANNY: *(Reading the cover.)* "Dingle Bells for Jesus."

DON: I believe it.

ROD: The name alone will sell tickets!

MANNY: Rod...

DON: No.

ROD: *(Hands Manny the spring script and takes back the Christmas script.)* And this is my Spring play. Wait till you hear this. Ok, so it's set in this gay bathhouse, in New York City, the village, Chelsea to be exact, it's spring, there's this straight guy hiding out from his brother-in-law who's in the mafia...

MANNY: Rod...

ROD: It's funny, it's brilliant, it's...

DON: "The Ritz!"

ROD: What?

DON: "The Ritz," Terrance McNally's play.

ROD: Really?

MANNY: Yes, Rod, we just watched that movie three weeks ago.

ROD: Oh, no wonder it sounded familiar. But wait, this is different, it's spring! It wasn't spring in that movie, no foliage. As a matter of fact it was raining.

DON: We can't do this.

ROD: Sure we can! Who cares about Terrance McNally? What smash hit did he ever write?

DON: "Lips Together Teeth Apart." *(retrieving his cell phone)*

ROD: Crap.

MANNY: Rod....

DON: "Love Valour Compassion." *(texting)*

ROD: Crap Crap Crap.

MANNY: Rod, we need to talk.

ROD: After Don reads my Christmas play.

DON: I don't want to read it. *(texting)*

ROD: Fine, don't read it. Terrence McNally, really?

DON: "Kiss of the Spider Woman."

ROD: Musical Crap.

MANNY: ROD! (*Don stops texting*)

ROD: (*looking at Manny*) Why so serious?

MANNY: Rod, a few weeks ago... (*Takes a deep breath.*) Don, well, Don and I (*Don begins texting*)

JIM: (*enters*) Hey guys. I have a question about this new kid.

ROD: What new kid?

MANNY: Jim, could you give us a moment?

JIM: The new guy, the playwright.

DON: Jim, a moment.

ROD: What new kid?

JIM: Is he a gay?

MANNY: Jim, can you please…

ROD: Is who a gay?

JIM: I mean, it's cool that I ask right?

ROD: (*To Manny.*) What the hell is he talking about?

MANNY: (*Sternly.*) Jim, I need to talk to Rod, do you mind?

JIM: Oh, oh yeah, sure thing. I'll be in the alley if you need me. (*Jim exits.*)

ROD: Ok, what's happening Manny?

MANNY: Rod, a few weeks ago... Don, well, Don and I…

ROD: Cut to the chase.

MANNY: We've found another play for the pageant this year.

ROD: You what?

DON: Rod, we had to do it. (*texting*)

JIM: (*enters*) Hey, anyone have a lighter?

MANNY: Not now Jim!

DON: (*To Jim, sternly.*) What do you need a lighter for?

JIM: Nothing. (*Tarquin enters with two costume sketches in hand.*)

TARQUIN: (*To Don.*) She know?

DON: Yep.

TARQUIN: Thank God! (*to Rod*) They fall off the edges, into the abyss…(*demonstrates fingers walking over the side of a cliff*) Ahhhhh…bye bye little untalented bitches. (*Tarquin exits.*)

ROD: (*Yelling off toward Tarquin.*) Your costumes suck!

TARQUIN: (*off*) Uninspired by the writing!

JIM: A lighter anyone?

MANNY: Jim, can you see we are in the middle of something?

JIM: Oh, the new playwright thing?

ROD: (*To Jim.*) How long have *you* known?

JIM: Known what?

DON: Jim! Take a break.

JIM: Oh cool, thanks. (*Jim exits.*)

ROD: So, gentlemen, who's my replacement.

DON: His name is M&M.

MANNY: He's not replacing you. He just wrote a good Christmas play. It's funny.

ROD: Oh really?

MANNY: Yes, you'll love it, trust me.

ROD: I doubt it.

JIM: (*enters.*) Hey, anyone have a lighter?

ROD: I think I've heard enough. I get it, Manny. You and Don made a decision without me, fine! (exits)

MANNY: That went well. *(To Don.)* Let's get some coffee.

DON: Actually (texting) I have to...

ROD: *(enters)* Did you both forget I'm one of the founding members of this theatre?

MANNY: No.

DON: How could we forg...

MANNY: *(interrupting)* Because I am!

DON: *(texting)* Young blood, Rod.

ROD: *(glares at Don)* Young blood?

DON: *(looking up from his phone)* That's what I said.

ROD: *(to Manny)* And you?

MANNY: I didn't say that.

ROD: *(back to Don)* So, It's all about the new younger blood, isn't it?

DON: Pretty much.

ROD: Fine Don. *(exits yelling)* I'll be in the box office, the dressing room, somewhere. Maybe find a place in this theatre where I belong. Possibly as the new charwoman.

TARQUIN: *(off)* Into the abyss!

ROD: *(off)* Shut up you inadequate hag!

JIM: What's a charwoman?

MANNY: *(looking up, noticing)* Jim, look at the Fresnel. It looks loose.

JIM: (looking) Yeah, I'll tighten it. *(he takes a lighter out of his pocket flicking it)*

DON: Make sure the safety cable's on.

JIM: Will do.

DON: *(to Manny pointing to lighter in Jims hand)* Look.

MANNY: *(to Jim)* You still need that lighter Jim?

JIM: Do you have one?

DON: No, but you do.

JIM: *(noticing the lighter in his hand)* Oh, wow. Like magic. *(to Don)* How did you do that?

DON: *(in disbelief to Manny)* Really, this is our tech guy? I have to go.

MANNY: I'll see you in an hour. (to Jim) Fix that light.

JIM: Got it!

(Manny and Don exit opposite directions as Jim opens his gay slang book.)

JIM: *(Reading.)* Additional gay slang: Hey Bitches. Approximate meaning: hello. Fabulous. Approximate meaning: fabulous. *(Jim exits. Sam enters. He's an attractive male in his twenties, very business minded in shirt and tie, notebook in hand. Removing his glasses he looks around.)*

SAM: *(To off stage right.)* It's clear. *(M&M enters. He is total Goth, sunglasses, high black boots, black pants, black shirt. He moves to center stage, looks around in silence for a few minutes, and after a long awkward pause, speaks.)*

M&M: I hate it.

SAM: I thought you might.

M&M: They're performing my Christmas play in this...

SAM: Yep.

M&M: Well, *(Resigned.)* let's go over the rules. Have your book?

SAM: Right here.

M&M: Read.

SAM: *(Opens book and begins reading.)* No rehearsals before 3:00 PM.

M&M: Check.

SAM: No line changes will be accepted.

M&M: Elucidate.

SAM: No ad libs.

M&M: Meaning?

SAM: Play must be presented word perfect.

M&M: As it should be. They wouldn't try to improve Shakespeare would they? *(Sam looks at M&M as they share a glance.)* Yes, you're right, *this shithole* probably would. Continue.

SAM: *(Reading from book.)* Brand name, purified bottled water at all rehearsals.

M&M: Meaning?

SAM: No generic crap.

M&M: Precisely. *(Jim enters, obviously stoned.)*

JIM: *(To M&M.)* Wow, what are you?

M&M: Excuse me?

JIM: Oh, wait, I came in here for something. What was it?

M&M: A brain? *(They share a laugh.)*

JIM: No. *(Suddenly stops laughing, remembering what it was.)* A lighter! *(Jim exits.)*

M&M: *(To Sam.)* What the hell was that? *(Back to business.)* Continue.

SAM: *(Reading from book.)* The playwright must have Director approval.

M&M: A ludicrous thing to have to ask.

SAM: Indeed.

M&M: Sam?

SAM: M? *(M&M removes his glasses and walks to center stage.)*

M&M: Do I sound like a Diva?

SAM: You do.

M&M: Perfect.

SAM: *(Looking at book.)* Shall I?

M&M: Continue.

SAM: *(Happily back in book.)* All royalties must be paid in full by… *(Tarquin enters with a tape measure, he stops and does a quick double take at M&M.)*

TARQUIN: What are we?

M&M: What?

TARQUIN: Exactly.

M&M: Excuse me?

TARQUIN: Why?

M&M: Huh?

TARQUIN: Oh gurl, I got no time for this. *(exits)*

JIM: (enters) Hello. (flicking lighter) either of you queens have a lighter?

M&M: *(To Sam)* Is he joking?

SAM: *(To Jim.)* Excuse me, what's your name?

JIM: Jim.

SAM: Jim, We represent the Christmas pageant.

JIM: The what?

SAM: *(Over annunciating.)* The Gayest Christ…

JIM: *(Interrupting)* Oh, gayest, you're in the right place.

SAM: Who are you?

JIM: The technical director, but, I'm straight.

SAM: Thank God. I'm Sam.

JIM: *(Smiles.)* Sam I am?

SAM: Excuse me?

JIM: *(Big smile.)* Sam I am. Dr. Seuss.

SAM: Are you stoned?

JIM: Are you?

SAM: You for real?

JIM: Sure am, girlfriend. *(snap)* Good, huh? I've been reading the book.

SAM: Book?

(Jim shows Sam the gay slag handbook as M&M looks on, Tarquin enters with a costume.)

M&M: *(Sarcastically.)* Gay slang...really?

TARQUIN: *(Speaking to M&M as he crosses.)* Representing.

M&M: *(to Tarquin)* What?

TARQUIN: No, I gotch you, *(giving him a quick once over)* girl be reppin for the low life. *(exits.)*

SAM: What did he say?

M&M: I'm clueless. *(to Jim.)* Listen, we're here to produce what is probably going to be the best Christmas production this theatre has ever seen.

JIM: Oh, you're the new guy?

M&M: I'm the playwright.

JIM: Right, okay, cool, they've been waiting for you. *(Yelling off stage.)* Manny, the new playwright is here! *(Both M&M and Sam stare at him for a moment. Jim tries to gay it up as Manny enters.)* I mean, the bitches are here, girl.

MANNY: *(Running in with coffee catching his breath.)* Jim! What are you doing?

JIM: Gay slang.

MANNY: Don't. *(He hands Jim the coffee as he crosses to Sam.)* Hello.

(Jim crosses behind M&M checking out his outfit. At this time he's removed the lid from the coffee.)

SAM: Good afternoon.

MANNY: So, you're the playwright.

SAM: No, *(motioning to M&M)* this is the playwright.

MANNY: Hello. *(Shakes M&M's hand.)* I'm Manny, the Assistant Producer. It's nice to finally meet you. Do you have any questions?

M&M: Are there any sane people here?

JIM: *(To M&M.)* Dude, are you a goth guy?

(As M&M turns, Jim accidentally spills coffee on his shoes.)

M&M: You idiot!

JIM: Oh man, sorry dude, my bad.

M&M: These are five hundred dollar designer shoes!

JIM: Seriously?! *(Pointing to his own shoes)* These were like fourteen bucks at Target.

M&M: I think you overpaid!

JIM: Dude, you too.

M&M: Are you serious?

JIM: I'm gagging. *(snap)* I'm doing good huh? *(on his gay slang)*

M&M: *(pause)* Sam, I'm done, let's go. *(exits)*

SAM: Um, Manny, was it?

MANNY: Yes, Manny.

SAM: That was Manuel Alfonso Martinez, M&M.

JIM: He's a playwright?

MANNY: He's *Mexican*?

SAM: Yes and yes, he wrote the play you were *going* to produce here, "The Gayest Christmas Pageant."

MANNY: Oh

SAM: I'm his Personal Assistant and we're pulling the rights.

MANNY: What?! You can't...we have a contract.

SAM: Oh yes, I have the unsigned copy right here. *(from his satchel)*

MANNY Unsigned?

SAM: Well look at that, it appears so.

MANNY: *(Lost for words.)* Shit.

SAM: I would.

JIM: Wow.

MANNY: This is bad.

SAM: You think?

MANNY: I forgot to sign it?

SAM: Yep.

MANNY: I can sign it now...

SAM: I think not.

JIM: Anything I can do?

SAM: I think you've done enough, girl. *(Snaps his fingers.)*

JIM: Good one.

SAM: I'm a natural.

MANNY: *(To Sam.)* Can you talk to him?

SAM: Nope.

MANNY: Please.

SAM: *(placing contact back in his satchel)* I love when they beg.

JIM: Sorry, I didn't mean to spill my coffee on his tacky shoes.

MANNY: Please.

SAM: It's fruitless. Have a nice day. *(Sam exits.)*

JIM: *(After a pause.)* Fruitless? *(looking it up)*

MANNY: *(Upset.)* Jim, what is that?

JIM: Slang.

MANNY: What?

JIM: *(Shows him the Gay Slang Handbook.)* See?

MANNY: "Gay Slang." What is this?

JIM: Just trying to fit in.

MANNY: *(Flipping through the book.)* Jim, not all gay people use these terms. Please, just be yourself.

JIM: Oh, cool *(pulling a joint out)* Wanna hit?

MANNY: No. What the hell Jim!

JIM: You said be myself.

MANNY: Well, stop it.

JIM: Should I go back to the book?

MANNY: No!

JIM: I'm confused.

MANNY: Just be yourself!

ROD: *(enters with his Christmas script in hand.)* You will be happy to know that I am over this little episode.

MANNY: Good.

JIM: *(to Rod)* Wanna hit? *(showing him the joint)*

ROD: Maybe.

MANNY: You don't smoke.

ROD: Maybe I should!

MANNY: You'd smoke pot?

ROD: Why not, things need to be shaken up around here.

MANNY: There's enough shaking going on already!

ROD: I disagree, that's why I personally invited Jim's mother to join us for the Christmas show this year.

JIM: What the fuck?

ROD: I know, don't thank me. She called asking for Jim, we talked, she laughed, said a few rude comments, I invited, she accepted, it's just that simple.

JIM: What the fuck?

ROD: What the fuck is right, why spend Christmas alone? She's in a cab on her way over.

JIM: What the…

MANNY: Rod, that's the last thing we need right now.

ROD: No, the last thing we need is another play slash playwright.

MANNY: Thanks to Jim we just lost our new play slash playwright.

ROD: *(Interested.)* Lost your play?

MANNY: Yes, Jim spilt his coffee...

JIM: Accidentally...but my Mom is…

ROD: Really? All of a sudden I love Jim.

MANNY: But you hate his mother.

JIM: Really?

ROD: No.

MANNY: Yes

ROD: Time to make amends.

JIM: Amends?

ROD: Why not?

JIM: Is that gay slang?

ROD: Look it up.

(Jim pulls out the Gay Slang book)

MANNY: *(sarcastically to Rod)* Amends?

ROD: Why not?

JIM: *(flipping through the book.)* Amends… amends…

MANNY: *(takes the book from Jim.)* Try a thesaurus.

ROD: Thesaurus?

JIM: A what?

MANNY: What are you trying to do, Rod?

ROD: Implying?

JIM: Clitoris?

MANNY: Get what you want?

ROD: What I want?

MANNY: *(handing book back to Jim.)* Yes, it's very P.A..

ROD: P.A.?

MANNY: Yes.

JIM: *(flipping through the book.)* P.A… P.A…

ROD: Who do you call when you're up the creek?

MANNY: No one's calling you, Rod.

JIM: *(Finding it.)* P.A. Prince Albert… Holy shit! *(Don and Tarquin enter.)*

DON: What the hell happened? I just ran into M&M. He walked out?

TARQUIN: *(to Rod)* What did you do bitch?

DON: What happened?

ROD: You all got what you deserved, trying to sneak behind by back!

DON: I wasn't sneaking behind your back.

MANNY: What to do now is the question.

DON: Cancel the Christmas pageant.

ROD: Cancel the pageant?

DON: Financially that's the safe choice.

ROD: You would cancel the show without even looking at my script?

MANNY AND DON: Yes!

ROD: I quit. QUIT! That's the last straw! *(exits and reenters quickly)* But you haven't heard the last of me! I'll get even one way or another! *(throws his script on the floor and exits.)*

TARQUIN: *(pause)* Only thing missing, the broomstick, puff of smoke and a loud cackle.

(Jim and Tarquin exit. Don and Manny look at each other then at Rod's script. Don picks up the script from the floor, walks up-stage, and sits. Manny joins him. Again they share a look. Both sigh as Don opens to the first page and they begin to read.)

FADE TO BLACKOUT.

END OF SCENE 1.

ACT 1
SCENE 2

Lights fade up. Don and Manny are still sitting as Manny finishes the last few pages of Rod's Christmas play. Don's coat now sits on the floor. Manny closes the script and they share a look of surprise.

MANNY: I don't believe it.
DON: Unbelievable.
MANNY: Rod's script.
DON: It's good. I would actually produce it.
MANNY: Shush!
DON: What is it?
MANNY: If we decide to produce it *after* telling Rod we *wouldn't…* Let's just say, he will make the whole process unbearable.
DON: Shit. What do we do?
MANNY: I'm thinking. *(Rod enters from up center holding the shitting Santa. He notices Manny with the script.)*
ROD: Ah ha! *(Rod grabs the script from Manny.)* So, you decided to read my play after all?
MANNY: Maybe.
ROD: And?
DON: It's a stupid title.
ROD: Then don't read it! *(Rod exits with script his in hand he stands just off listening)*
DON: We have to do his play.
MANNY: How? *(Jim enters.)*
JIM: Hey guys, great news! Guess who's here? My mother! Yeah, dude. MY MOTHER! *(sacastily)* I can't believe I get to spend some quality time this Christmas with my mom. *(Thinking about this for a moment)* Thanks a lot Rod! I need a hit. *(Jim takes joint out of his pocket and exits.)*
DON: What's up with that?
MANNY: You ever meet Jim's mother?
DON: No.
MANNY: She's charming. Hey wait a minute, this is great! Rod invited Jim's Mother, and since he'll have to deal with her… this might work… I'll hire a director…
DON: Don't you think he'll catch on when he sees us producing his play?
MANNY: Here's the thing, we change the title, have the new director tweak it a little, and Rod's none the wiser. The only thing we need to do is keep him busy.
MONICA: *(From offstage.)* Where the hell is everybody? Jim!
MANNY: And I think I hear the person who will take care of that problem for us. *(Rod enters unseen as Monica, an older woman in her eighties, enters with a walker and is dressed shabbily wearing a MAGA hat and covered in pro Trump pins. There is a dim light in the alley where Jim is smoking a joint.)*
DON: Who is that?
MANNY: Jim's mother, Monica.
MONICA: Any of you fags see my son?
DON: Oh boy.
MANNY: *(Crossing to Monica.)* Hi Monica.
MONICA: Who the hell are you?

MANNY: Manny, we met last fall.

MONICA: I don't remember you. Where the hell is my son?

MANNY: I think he stepped outside.

MONICA: Probably smoking that peyote.

MANNY: Possibly.

MONICA: It's the only way he can keep his sanity, working with fags.

DON: That's offensive.

MONICA: What is?

DON: The word "fags." We prefer gay.

MONICA: Gay?! Gay…when I was a kid gay meant happy. You people are not happy! Fruitcakes, stealing all the nice words and making them *perverted.*

DON: I'm happy.

MONICA: Bull shit!

DON: Hey, you don't know me.

MONICA: And I don't want to.

DON: You're right Manny, she's charming.

MONICA: Where's my son?

DON: Getting a P.A.

MANNY: Don!

MONICA: A what?

MANNY: *(Trying to lighten the mood.)* Nothing Monica. Don's just being funny.

MONICA: I don't get it!

DON: I don't think you can.

MONICA: What?

MANNY: Don!

DON: What? She's a bigot!

MONICA: *(Crossing upstage.)* One hour in a cab! An hour! Damn cab driver smelled like crap. Looked like he fell out of bed, still had the pillowcase on his head!

DON: *(Can't believe what he's hearing.)* Are you kidding me?

MONICA: No! I just spent my whole social security check on a damn cab ride! Then pillow head asked for a tip! I'm done! BUILD THAT WALL! *(as a side note)* One of you pansies *will* drive me home.

DON: Trump is a douchebag. *(There's tension in the air and a silent awkward pause.)*

MONICA: *(Monica breaks the quiet via Tourette's.)* Faggot, faggot, faggot, fag, fag, shit… *(She continues under the next exchange.)*

DON: *(Going for her.)* That's it!

MANNY: *(Stopping Don.)* No, it's the Tourette's

DON: Tourette's?

MONICA: Shit, shit, shit, shit, fag, shit, fuck, shit, fag, fag, fag. build that wall, lock her up *(Monica stops then passes out, falling to the floor. Manny and Don stare for a moment.)*

MANNY: *(Calmly.)* Did I mention narcoleptic?

JIM: *(enters from the alley obviously stoned.)* Hello Manny, Don, Mom, Rod. Anyone else have the munchies?

DON: Jim, your Mother's on the floor.

JIM: *(Jim looks but has no reaction.)* She sure is. *(To Manny.)* Do you have any chips in your office?

MANNY: No.

JIM: Candy?

MANNY: No.

JIM: Ice cream?

DON: Are you high?

JIM: Depends.

DON: On?

JIM: Are you?

DON: No.

JIM: Then neither am I. *(Monica starts to groan.)*

MANNY: Oh no.

JIM: I don't feel good. I need to eat something. *(Jim exits upstage. Monica starts to sit up as Don and Manny lean over her.)*

MANNY: You all right Monica?

MONICA: What the hell happened? Did you two try to rape me?

DON: You wish!

MONICA: I want to go home. *(She stands up.)*

MANNY: I'll find Jim. Why don't you lie down and relax in the dressing room. *(Monica starts to exit stage left.)*

MONICA: I knew this was a bad idea. I should have never listened to that queer Rod. *(Imitating Rod.)* Come here for Christmas, have a nice time, why spend it alone? An hour in a cab…This place smells like a urinal. Someone get me my hemorrhoid pillow! *(Monica exits.)*

MANNY: *(To Don.)* What next? *(Manny and Don exit stage right. Jim enters from stage left eating a bag of potato chips. Rod quickly enters from up center.)*

ROD: *(To Jim.)* You! Do you have any idea what's going on right now? *(Jim's mouth is full of chips. He shakes his head no.)* I'm being plagiarized by my own lover. *(Jim tries to talk but is incomprehensive.)* What? What!

JIM: *(Swallows.)* I have no idea what plag-it-tised means.

ROD: Plagiarized. In this case it means stealing someone else's play, without my acknowledgement.

JIM: Really?

ROD: Yes, really.

JIM: I can't believe that.

ROD: Tell me about it.

JIM: Harsh.

ROD: To say the least.

JIM: You have any chocolate on you?

ROD: Sure, let me pull it out of my ass.

JIM: Nevermind.

(Note: The following dialogue is at a rapid pace with both actors not really hearing the other until Jim mentions the Fresnel.)

ROD: They read my play Jim. Read it and liked it!

JIM: Who they?

ROD: They want to change the title, hire a director!

JIM: Do you really have chocolate in your ass?

ROD: They're not getting away with this, it's my play.

JIM: *(Reacting to chocolate in the ass.)* That's gotta' hurt.

ROD: I started this theatre.

JIM: *(Looking up.)* I thought I fixed that Fresnel.

ROD: My ideas, my hard work, you think it's easy to write a play?

JIM: I can't spell very well. *(About the Fresnel.)* It looks loose.

ROD: I'll show them. I'll cast the play and direct it!

JIM: I'm going to fix that Fresnel, Rod.

ROD: I could care less, let it fall on someone's head.

JIM: I'll be back. *(Jim exits. Rod moves center stage.)*

ROD: Make a monkey out of me, will you? *(Jim can be heard climbing a ladder back stage.)* Steal my play? This is how they treat someone after years of devotion and talent? You heartless people. Christmas, it's supposed to be a time of love, caring, giving. *(Rod looks up.)* Jim? What are you doing? Jesus! Jesus!

JIM: Heads up! *(Rod screams.)*

SNAP TO BLACKOUT.

LOUD CRASH.

A bright light shines on center stage, focused on Jesus holding his arms out. A loud chorus is singing "Hallelujah Chorus."

SNAP TO BLACKOUT.

END OF SCENE 2.

ACT 1
SCENE 3

Lights fade up on Don, Manny and Jim standing center stage.

DON: Jesus Christ!
MANNY: Jim, how did that light fall?
JIM: I'm not sure, last thing I remember I was eating a bag of chips...
MANNY: We have to make sure *all* the lights have safety cables, Jim.
JIM: *(Suddenly remembers.)* That's what I was trying to do.
DON: Is he at home now?
MANNY: Yes, he's on prescription painkillers, enough to see Jesus.
DON: I'm glad he's ok.
MANNY: He's fine, except for the stitches and slight concussion.
JIM: *(Explodes.)* Dude, I'm so sorry!
MANNY: Just thank God you didn't kill him.
MONICA: *(Yelling from offstage.)* Where the hell is everybody? *(They all look quickly off towards Monica's voice.)*
MANNY: Jim, your mother.
DON: What the hell are we going to do with her?
JIM: I think at this point…
MONICA: *(From off stage.)* Faggies, where are you?
JIM: Sorry about that.
DON: She's a work of art.
JIM: I'll send her back home.
MANNY: That might not be a bad idea.
JIM: Understood. *(Monica enters.)*
MONICA: Are you deaf? Didn't you hear me? *(To Manny.)* Hello Danny.
MANNY: It's Manny.
MONICA: *(To Don as if hello.)* Pansy.
DON: *(Responding in the same tone.)* Bigot.
MONICA: *(To Jim.)* I want to go home!
JIM: Ok mom, we're in the middle of something now.
MONICA: Are they trying to convert you?
DON: We don't need him.
MANNY: No one's converting anyone here.
MONICA: *(Monica pulls book from Jim's back pocket.)* Then what's this?
JIM: *(Jim takes the book back.)* I bought that mom.
MONICA: Where, from their faggoty gift store?
MANNY: We don't have a gift store.
DON: Not a bad idea though, faggoty gift store.
JIM: Mom, I'll take care of getting you back home when we're done.
MONICA: Fine. I'll be out in the lobby if anyone is interested.
DON: I doubt anyone is.
MANNY: Don!

MONICA: Jesus will get you for that.

MANNY: I thought you were an atheist?

MONICA: I thought you were a man.

JIM: MOM! That's enough, this is my job! Now go sit in the lobby!

MONICA: I'm going, no need to raise your voice. *(starts to exit.)* Rude people….rude…. and I never said I was an atheist! *(exits.)*

DON: Rude? She thinks *we're* rude, please... *(To Jim)* I'm sorry, your mother pushes my buttons.

JIM: Mine, too.

DON: I think she finds ones I never even knew I had.

JIM: I hear you girl. *(Snaps his fingers.)*

DON: *(Giving Jim a strange look.)* So, Manny, the Christmas pageant, what now?

MANNY: We do Rod's play.

DON: Who's going to direct it?

MANNY: It's taken care of. At the hospital I took a minute to call a lesbian friend of mine who's a brilliant director. She flew in from New York.

DON: New York?!

MANNY: She flew in on her dime Don, not ours. She's here on vacation visiting family. We just have to pay her for taking the time to do this on her vacation.

DON: When do we meet her?

MANNY: In two hours.

DON: Great! The pageant is on!

MANNY: It is.

DON: Let's draw up a contract.

MANNY: Good idea.

DON: And sign it this time!

MANNY: I get it Don, don't rub it in.

DON: Taking a dinner break Jim?

JIM: No, no, I ate a whole bag of chips… I'll stay here. I have stuff I need to finish.

MANNY: Double check and make sure all the lights have safety cables on them.

JIM: I'm on it.

DON: And don't kill anybody...unless it's your mother.

JIM: Huh, that's funny. *(Manny and Don exit as Jim continues.)* Don't worry guys I'm on it…I've got lots of stuff to keep me busy. *(reaches into his shirt pocket, pulls out a joint addressing it)* Hello stuff. *(He sits on the box up center and lights the joint. After a moment Jesus enters. He stands with his arms stretched from side to side. After a moment Jim notices Jesus, he slowly rubs his eyes, looks again, then at the joint.)*

JIM: This is some good cheap shit! *(He pauses.)* Jesus?

JESUS: Jim.

JIM: *The* Jesus?

JESUS: Yes… *(With a Hispanic accent.)* Jesús. *(Jesus sits next to Jim. Jim is lost for words. They both stare forward motionless for a few minutes. Jim very slowly raises his hand to offers Jesus the joint. they both continue to look forward)*

JIM: Wanna hit?

JESUS: No, thank you. *(After a pause, Jim touches Jesus on the arm. Jesus looks at him.)*

JIM: Sorry, just making sure.

JESUS: I understand.

JIM: So, Jesus, you're not drug induced?

JESUS: Nope.

JIM: *(Nervous laugh.)* Oh good, man I thought I'd OD'd on pot.
JESUS: Not yet.
(They share a laugh)
JIM: *(sudden and seriously)* You mean I will?
JESUS: No.
(They share a laugh)
JIM: Good, you scared me… I mean… the fact… you know all and see all. I didn't think you *can* OD on pot. *(Jim pauses.)* Why are you here?
JESUS: Business.
JIM: Business?
JESUS: Yes.
JIM: Oh cool. Do you always dress like that?
JESUS: Only when I first appear to people.
JIM: Why?
JESUS: So you might know me, my son.
JIM: That's a good idea. *(Jim Pauses.)* Do you know some people see your face in a tortilla?
JESUS: Really?
JIM: Yeah. *(Jim pauses.)* This is so cool. I'm chilling with Jesus.
JESUS: I'm chilling with myself. *(Jesus smiles.)*

FADE TO BLACKOUT.

END OF SCENE 3.

ACT 1
SCENE 4

As lights fade up a director's table is placed stage left, with four chairs placed behind it. A keyboard and bench or chair sit stage right. After a moment, Janet, a young assistant director in her twenties, wearing a "RESIST" t-shirt enters, carrying a stack of headshots and resumes. She places them on the table and starts to organize them. Enter Margie, an attractive African American in her late thirties or early forties. She has a cup of coffee in her hand as she looks out at the house.

MARGIE: *(Making a statement.)* No wonder they have no money.
JANET: Excuse me?
MARGIE: Nothing. Actually I was commenting on the size of the theater.
JANET: You're just used to those large New York theaters.
MARGIE: Not all theaters in New York are large. You ever been?
JANET: Where? Oh, you mean New York? No, someday I hope.
MARGIE: So what's the plan?
JANET: All auditioners will have a prepared monologue and will sing sixteen measures of a Broadway or Christmas song.
MARGIE: Why? It's not a musical.
JANET: Well, there's some singing involved.
MARGIE: *(Remembering disappointedly.)* Oh yeah, *that*. Do we have an accompanist?
JANET: Oh, yes. Martha. She plays all our shows.
MARGIE: Well, where is she?
JANET: Taking a nap in the dressing room.
MARGIE: Shouldn't we wake her up?
JANET: Oh no, one good thing about Martha, she's very punctual. I told her we needed her at three o'clock sharp and that means *(Janet look at her watch.)* she will be in three… two… one. *(Martha enters. She is a little old lady in her nineties, dressed casually with a long white shawl. She carries a very large satchel overflowing with sheet music, pens, paper, box of tissues, mints and a fly swatter. She walks quickly to the keyboard. Suddenly she stops and farts.)*
MARGIE: Excuse me? Hello? *(Martha is undaunted and continues walking, stopping once again to fart.)*
MARGIE: *(Upset.)* Hello!
JANET: Oh, she's a little hard of hearing. *(Martha sits down at the keyboard. She sees Janet and Margie. For the first time she smiles and waves, then suddenly lays her head down on the piano keys, and is fast asleep.)*
JANET: *(Under her breath.)* Like I said, punctual.
MARGIE: *(Margie pulls Janet aside.)* Come here.
JANET: What is it?
MARGIE: Well?
JANET: What?
MARGIE: Come on, are you in on this?
JANET: In on what?
MARGIE: This is a joke right?
JANET: A joke?

MARGIE: Manny's trying to get even, right?

JANET: What?

MARGIE: Ok, I admit, I shouldn't have invited them to New York, then kicked them out of my apartment the second day after they arrived, but that was seven years ago, they should be over it by now.

JANET: What are you talking about?

MARGIE: Come on, they told you that story.

JANET: I'm afraid not.

MARGIE: They came to New York on a short vacay, and I stupidly invited them to stay at my place. I had a one bedroom apartment at the time, and between Manny's loud snoring and Rod's singing in the shower at eight in the morning, I couldn't take it anymore, and neither could my upstairs neighbors. Let's not even get into the *loud* late night sex acts. Anyway, I had no choice but to ask them to leave. It was too much. I was directing a show at the time, it was a big deal, my first real break, I couldn't sleep. Get the picture?

JANET: I think so.

MARGIE: So I politely asked them to leave, to get a hotel room. *(Margie picks up the script.)* And now this, *(Margie points to Martha.)* and that, is payback, right?

JANET: I'm lost.

MARGIE: Did you read this?

JANET: Not yet.

MARGIE: You agreed to assistant direct a play you never read.

JANET: No.

MARGIE: No?

JANET: No, I mean yes.

MARGIE: Now I'm lost.

JANET: I haven't read this play yet. You had the only copy.

MARGIE: I see. Well let's get some additional copies, ok?

JANET: I'll take care of it.

MARGIE: It sucks!

JANET: Excuse me?

MARGIE: This play, are all his plays this bad?

JANET: No comment.

MARGIE: Why is that?

JANET: Listen, I've worked with Rod for the past three years, and I keep my personal opinions about his playwriting to myself.

MARGIE: Why?

JANET: Because I love this job. Sure it's part time work, but it's what I love to do, theatre. It may be a small, crappy, amateurish community theater where almost everyone is gay, *(Janet looks at Margie.)* or a lesbian, or a pothead *(Janet looks at Martha.)* or close to death. But, I'm open-minded. They respect me, treat me nice, pay me what they can afford, I do my job, *very well* I might add, and keep my opinions to myself. I mean, it's subjective anyway, right?

MARGIE: *(Referring to the script.)* NO, this sucks!

JANET: *(Emotionless.)* Big surprise.

MARGIE: I can't direct this!

JANET: What?! Wait, you have to! You already said you would.

MARGIE: How? Something's up. No person in their right mind could read this crap and think it's good.

JANET: You'd be surprised.

MARGIE: Is that an opinion?

JANET: No!

MARGIE: I can't direct this crap.

JANET: Margie, you have to. They're your friends.

MARGIE: Not really. Kind'a friends of a friend.

JANET: Please, theatre funds are low, they need this pageant, and I need this job.

MARGIE: Can't you assist another director?

JANET: I could, but do you know how good this would look on my resume, to add that I actually worked with a professional New York director.

MARGIE: In a really shitty play, oh yeah, who wouldn't hire you after that.

JANET: Please, Margie. *You* can make this play good.

MARGIE: God couldn't help that.

JANET: Consider it a learning experience.

MARGIE: *(taken back)* A what?

JANET: *(correcting)* For me.

MARGIE: How can I make this good? I mean, yes, it's the birth of Christ, but then it jumps to some gay shit with some Brokeback mountain cowboys as shepherds.

JANET: Look, Margie, I know it's strange, and I really don't know you well enough to ask for a personal favor, but I would love just one opportunity to work with a real professional New York director. *(Margie looks at Janet, then at Martha.)*

MARGIE: Oh Lord what did I get myself into?

JANET: Please?

MARGIE: Ok. Damn it.

JANET: Great!

MARGIE: But, if I find out this is a joke and you're part of it, I'll personally make sure you never work in this or any city again. Deal?

JANET: Deal.

MARGIE: This *(Margie holds up the script.)* is going to need a miracle.

JANET: May we begin?

MARGIE: You really want to do this?

JANET: I do.

MARGIE: I don't believe this.

JANET: Believe. We have actors waiting.

MARGIE: All right, just let the coffee kick in. *(Manny enters followed by Don.)*

MANNY: Janet, you have everything you need?

JANET: I believe so.

MANNY: *(To Margie.)* Thank you so much for doing this for us.

MARGIE: *(Looking at Janet.)* No problem.

DON: And accepting the meager salary.

MARGIE: It paid for my trip. *(To Manny)* How's Rod?

MANNY: Better.

MARGIE: Glad to hear it.

MANNY: Have you met our technical director and costumer?

MARGIE: No, I haven't.

MANNY: I'll go get them. *(Margie pulls Manny aside.)*

MARGIE: Manny, Manny, Manny… did Rod really write this play?

MANNY: That's what he tells me.

MARGIE: It's good.

MANNY: We thought so.

MARGIE: *(Sarcastically.)* I mean the entire concept. Mary, Joseph the birth of Christ, it's refreshing.

MANNY: *(Clueless.)* Yes, has a great message.

MARGIE: I know, I think I've heard it before.

MANNY: Maybe from the Bible?

MARGIE: That's it. *Almost* word for word, except for the gay shit.

MANNY: Let me find Jim and Tarquin.

MARGIE: *(Margie speaks to house.)* I don't even want to know what a Tarquin is. *(Manny exits.)*

JANET: *(To Margie.)* We have to begin the audition process.

MARGIE: *(Referring to Martha.)* You better wake up Grandma. And please, keep this on schedule.

JANET: That's my job. *(Janet crosses to Martha and speaks to her loudly.)* Martha! Martha!

MARTHA: What? What is it?

JANET: We're going to begin.

MARTHA: *(Happy.)* A shot of Gin?

JANET: *(Speaking very loud.)* No, we are starting the audition!

MARTHA: Ok, ok, no need to yell! *(Martha sits up, picks up the fly swatter, hits a fly on the keyboard, then turns it on.)*

MARGIE: *(To Don.)* You know where I can get another cup of this coffee?

DON: Allow me.

MARGIE: You have anything stronger?

DON: No. Sorry.

MARGIE: Me too. *(Don takes her cup and exits. Janet picks a few resumes and starts to exit, then turns to Margie.)*

JANET: Thank you, for doing this.

MARGIE: No problem.

JANET: And don't you worry, I can be a *real bitch* if I have to be. *(Margie looks at Janet in horror as Janet exits. Martha's head falls back on the keys, causing a loud steady flow of the cords. Margie looks up to the ceiling.)*

MARGIE: Oh Jesus, help us all.

FADE TO BLACKOUT.

END SCENE 4.

ACT 1
SCENE 5

Lights fade up on Actor One, standing center stage. Janet, Margie, Manny, and Don (texting) sit stage right behind the director's table. A large group of actors including Mary, Joseph, and Tyrone are seen in the alley, pacing, rehearsing their monologues, some hold headshots, others are texting.

ACTOR ONE: Do we have to slate?

JANET: It's stage, not film.

ACTOR ONE: Is that a no? *(Martha suddenly starts to play a song and the actor lets out a slight scream of surprise.)*

JANET: Martha NO! *(Martha stops playing.)*

MARTHA: What?

JANET: Not yet.

MARTHA: When then?

JANET: I'll let you know.

MARTHA: How much longer?

JANET: I'll tell you when!

MARTHA: This is insane.

JANET: *(To Actor One.)* Continue.

ACTOR ONE: What?

JANET: Continue.

ACTOR ONE: Continue? I never started.

JANET: Well, start already!

ACTOR ONE: *(Flustered, Actor One takes a breath and begins.)* To be or not to be... *(Jim enters and crosses in front of Actor One.)*

MANNY: Jim, where the hell have you been?

ACTOR ONE: *(Flustered.)* That is the question.

JIM: Talking to Jesus.

MANNY: Never mind that, this is Margie, our new director.

JIM: Hey.

MARGIE: Jim.

MANNY: And you know Janet.

JIM: *(Cold.)* Hello.

JANET: *(Cold.)* Whatever.

MARGIE: Did you say you were talking to Jesus?

JIM: I was.

MANNY: *(Nervous laugh.)* Jim's been praying a lot since he dropped...

ACTOR ONE: *(Interrupting.)* Excuse me?

MANNY: What?

ACTOR ONE: May I continue?

MANNY: Oh yes, sorry. *(Jim stands and watches.)*

ACTOR ONE: *(Completely thrown off.)* 'tis a consummation Devoutly to be wish'd. To die, to sleep... *(Remembering where he was.)* to sleep, perchance to dream.

JIM: What the hell is this?

MARGIE: Shakespeare.

ACTOR ONE: *(Distracted.)* No more; and by a sleep to say we end… *(Tarquin enters and Actor One stops.)*

MANNY: Tarquin!

TARQUIN: I'm pissed.

DON: Why?

TARQUIN: When was I going to be told the play changed?

ACTOR ONE: I'd hate to interrupt…

TARQUIN: *(Faces Actor One.)* Then don't. *(To Manny and Don.)* Well?

MANNY: Margie, this is your costumer.

TARQUIN: Who's she?

MANNY: The director.

TARQUIN: Of what?

MANNY: The new play.

DON: …that *Manny* forgot to tell you about.

MANNY: Me?

TARQUIN: Ok, you know what? I can't work this way. I quit!

DON: You can't!

TARQUIN: Watch me!

DON: We paid for those costumes in full!

TARQUIN: And you can keep them! *(Exits.)*

ACTOR ONE: *(After a beat.)* Excuse me.

DON AND MANNY: What?!

JANET: Guys, maybe we should take a break?

JIM: *(Overly happy.)* Yes.

MARGIE: No. We have actors waiting. Let's get these auditions over with.

JANET: *(To Actor One.)* Continue!

ACTOR ONE: *(confused)* What?

DON: Continue.

ACTOR ONE: Ok, is there anyone else dropping by? *(Everyone glares at Actor One for a moment and he continues.)* To be or not to be…That is the question! *(Everyone moans and shifts positions. Tarquin enters with both arms full of costumes, drops them on the stage and exits. Actor One ignores Tarquin, pauses to find his place, has no idea, but continues.)* Ay, there's the rub..

JIM: *(Trying to be funny.)* A dub, dub.

ACTOR ONE: For in that sleep of death what dreams may come…

JIM: Wow...that's heavy.

ACTOR ONE: *(To Jim)* I'm sorry…am I interrupting?

JIM: No.

ACTOR ONE: Good…For in that sleep…

DON: Uh…

ACTOR ONE: What!

DON: Do you have anything contemporary?

ACTOR ONE: You haven't even paid me any attention, your texting!

DON: Is that a no?

ACTOR ONE: YES!

DON: So yes it's a no?

ACTOR ONE: What?

DON: I'll take it as a no.

ACTOR ONE: No, No, NO! Know what… this isn't working for me. This isn't an audition, it's a circus. When you people get your shit together then call me…. ok! *(begins to exit.)*
JANET: So we'll see you at callbacks?
ACTOR ONE: *(Matter of factly.)* Of course. *(exits as Jim starts to pick up the costumes.)*
JANET: *(Teasing.) Hey* Jim, you auditioning or here to drop a light on someone's head?
JIM: Hey, not funny!
MARGIE: *You're* responsible for Rod's vacation?
JIM: It was an accident.
JANET: *(To Margie.)* And, he's building our set.
MARGIE: May we continue?
JANET: Yes, Jim, *on your way out,* send in the next actor.
JIM: What number you on?
JANET: Two. That's one plus one.
JIM: *(Looks at Janet.)* Cold. *(Jim exits.)*
MARGIE: *(to Janet)* Girl, you are cruel.
JANET: He's a flake.
MARGIE: You like him, huh?
JANET: In his dreams.

Tina enters. She is an attractive woman in her late thirties, the diva, and every word is pushed out with a pretentious smile. She carries a colorful cloth bag. She has the number nine pinned to her shirt. Janet reacts to Tina, who she secretly dislikes, and to the wrong number.

TINA: Hello.
MARGIE: Hello.
DON: Hi.
TINA: Hi Don.
MANNY: Ola.
TINA: Ola Manny. *(Looking for Rod.)* Rod's not directing?
MANNY: Don't ask. This is Margie, the director.
TINA: *(Overly pretentious.)* Hello.
MARGIE: Hey.
JANET: Name?
TINA: Janet, you know my name.
JANET: Name!
TINA: Tina, same as it was last audition. *(Everyone laughs except Janet.)*
JANET: Last name.
TINA: Oh poo, Janet, you know that too.
MARGIE: Did you prepare a monologue?
TINA: I did.
JANET: Go ahead.
TINA: Just do my monologue?
JANET: Please.
TINA: Oh, ok. I would like to recite a monologue from the NBC Emmy Award-winning daytime drama "Days of Our Lives." *(Janet groans.)*
MARGIE: An interesting choice.
TINA: Why thank you…
MARGIE: Margie.

TINA: Margie. *(Tina takes a moment to get into character, turning away, and making a loud squeal, suddenly facing forward and over-acting the entire monologue.)* What is life? Is life simply the aspect of existence? A meager processes of acts, and reacts that evaluates and evolves? Or is life simply anything that grows and eventually dies? NO! LIfe is family...family Jake.....it was my father's only wish that I would not be present when all this turmoil happens. How can we treat each other this way! We are family, did you hear me Jake, FAMILY! And I know it was you who killed my only Son! My ONLY son, from my fourth marriage. How could you.. I loved you, Jake! You are my brother. and FAMILY! But now.....I don't know, I can't go on... this stress is too much. My heart, my heart, I can't breathe... Oh no...It seems I'm dying...Did you hear me Jake ... Dying! Dying... Dying...I'm dy... *(Tina falls to the floor. Don and Manny stand and clap loudly. Margie is dumbfounded.)*

MANNY: That gets better every time I hear it.

TINA: You are so kind.

MANNY: Tina was our Laurie in Okla-Homo!

TINA: It was my first token lesbian role.

MARGIE: I didn't know there was a lesbian role in Oklahoma.

MANNY: There isn't in Oklaho-*ma. (Manny and Don high-five.)*

MARGIE: *(To Janet.)* What the...

JANET: Don't ask. *(To Tina.)* You have a song prepared?

TINA: I do, let me get my music. *(Tina takes music out of her bag and crosses to Martha. She speaks loudly.)* Hello Martha!

MARTHA: Hello Tina.

TINA: *(Louder.)* How are you today?

MARTHA: I was fine till you started shouting in my damn ears! *(Tina hands Martha the sheet music and crosses back. After a moment Martha starts to play "Tomorrow" from "Annie." Everyone moans and shifts positions.)*

TINA: *(Singing.)* Theee...

MARGIE: *(Stands and interrupts Tina.)* THANK YOU. *(Martha stops playing.)*

TINA: *(Annoyed.)* I didn't sing yet.

MARGIE: I know.

TINA: Well, how do you know I can?

MARGIE: I'll take your word for it.

TINA: *(Sincerely.)* Oh, well... that's very nice. Thank you.

MARGIE: You're welcome. We'll be calling people tonight and letting them know.

JANET: Thank you.

MANNY: Thanks Tina.

TINA: Ok, well, thank you all. Tell Rod hello.

MANNY: I will. *(Tina starts to exit.)*

JANET: NEXT! (Startled Tina drops her handbag)

MARGIE: Jesus girl! You scared the shit out of me. Inside voice. *(Spike enters with number eleven on his shirt, Janet reacts. As he brushes past he bumps into Tina.)*

SPIKE: *(To Tina.)* Excuse you. *(They give each other a cold glare. He carries four cheesy headshots, walks directly to the table and hands them individually to Janet, Margie, Manny and Don, and plants himself center stage posed and ready to audition. Tina watches from off right.)*

JANET: Name?

SPIKE: Fromage!

JANET: Excuse me?

SPIKE: Fromage!

DON: *(Laughing as he looks at Spike's headshot.)* That's French for cheese. *(Spike glares at Don.)*

SPIKE: It's a stage name.

MARGIE: What's your real name?

SPIKE: Spike! *(Everyone laughs and Spike quickly interrupts.)* I would like to recite a monologue from the NBC Emmy Award-winning daytime drama "Days of Our Lives."

MANNY/DON: What?!

MARGIE: You go girl. *(Spike turns and gives a look to Tina as if to say "watch this bitch.")*

SPIKE: What is life? Is life simply the aspect of existence? A meager processes of acts, and reacts that evaluates and evolves? Or is life simply anything that grows and eventually dies? NO! LIfe is family...family Jake…..it was my father's only wish that I would not be present when all this turmoil happens. How can we treat each other this way! We are family, did you hear me Jake, FAMILY! And I know it was you who killed my only Son! My ONLY son, from my fourth marriage. How could you.. I loved you, Jake! You are my brother. and FAMILY! But now…..I don't know, I can't go on... this stress is too much. My heart, my heart, I can't breathe… Oh no...It seems I'm dying…Did you hear me Jake … Dying! Dying... Dying...I'm dy...*(wipes the stage as not to dirty his shirt.)* Dying! *(falls to the floor. Margie stands applauding as the others sit arms folded.)*

MARGIE: We will be calling you tonight!

SPIKE: I know. *(Spike exits followed by Tina as Tyrone enters. He is a black man from the hood in his early thirties, gangster attitude, chewing gum, wearing a "Hi Hater" t-shirt and a do-rag with the number three pinned on it.)*

JANET: *(Noticing it's the wrong number.)* Mother fuck... *(To Margie.)* Jim can't count. *(To Tyrone.)* Name?

TYRONE: Tyrone.

JANET: Are you chewing gum?

TYRONE: *(Aggressive.)* You got a problem with that?

JANET: *(Backing off.)* No.

TYRONE: Good. *(Speaking under his breath.)* Cracker bitch.

JANET: Excuse me?

TYRONE: What?

JANET: Did you say something?

TYRONE: Why, did you hear something?

JANET: No.

TYRONE: Good.

MARGIE: Do you have a monologue?

TYRONE: *(Tyrone smiles very flirtatious at Margie.)* I do, just holler at your boy.

JANET: What?

MARGIE: *(Impatiently.)* Just do it.

TYRONE: I got this monologue, two weeks ago, off Craigslist. *(Performing the entire monologue aggressively.)* I have approximately 200 cinder blocks for sale. They are standard 8"x8"x16". They cost me about buck seven de five if you get them someplace else. I'm asking fifty cents a block. You pick them up and you move them yourself. Please don't waste my fucking time with endless emails. These are plain old cinder blocks, for fuck sake. Now listen, we are all busy people here. You want the blocks? Come get the fucking blocks and give me fifty cents for every block you take. How fucking hard is that? I just want to get these fucking things off my property. So if you want them, get the fuck over here with some money and take them. The next fucking moron that emails me with "I'm building a blah blah blah, and was wondering if…" The answer is NO. Come get the fucking blocks and build it yourself. What the fuck is wrong with you people? The next one of you fucking jackasses that emails me with some sob story bullshit is getting his email address added to the North American Man/Boy Love Association

mailing list. You want the blocks? Come get the blocks, *(Tyrone leans aggressively over Janet who cowers.)* and don't fuck with me! *(Tyrone smiles. Everyone stares silently at Tyrone in disbelief.)*
JANET: *(lost)* Thank you? *(Jim enters with Actor Three holding a ventriloquist puppet dressed as Santa Claus. Actor Three has the number three pinned on his shirt. Janet and Margie haven't noticed them yet; they are looking at Tyrone's resume and headshot.)*

Note: Actor Three is shy, soft spoken and awkward. His alter ego is the Santa Clause, and should be the complete opposite.

TYRONE: *(To Actor Three.)* What's up?
ACTOR THREE: Nothing brother.
TYRONE: I'm not your brother.
JANET: Jim, don't you see we have someone in here auditioning?
JIM: I do. *(Margie looks up and notices Santa.)*
MARGIE: What the hell is that?
JIM: I think it's Santa.
MARGIE: You *think?*
JANET: *(To Actor Three.)* Is that Santa with you?
ACTOR THREE: It is.
TYRONE: Bullshit, Santa's black.
ACTOR THREE: Really?
TYRONE: He is in *my* hood.
MARGIE: *(Jokingly.)* Santa, you auditioning?
ACTOR THREE: *(Covering the puppets mouth.)* No!
MARGIE: *(Laughs.)* I'm asking Santa.
JANET: *(Joins in.)* Does Santa speak?
ACTOR THREE: He can, please don't ask him to!
MARGIE: *(To Janet.)* Can you believe this?
JANET: Hardly.
MARGIE: *(To Manny.)* What kind of circus you running here, Manny?
MANNY: *I've* never seen anything like this before. *(Alex, a pizza delivery girl, enters. She is butch, dressed like a boy and carrying a large pizza box.)*
ALEX: Who ordered the large pepperoni?
DON: Over here! *(Margie gives him a look.)* What? I was hungry.

Martha hits a cord by mistake making a loud sound. Everyone jumps. At the exact same time, Jesus walks in, unnoticed by everyone except Jim. Jesus is wearing a t-shirt that reads "What would I do?" Tyrone pulls a gun and Alex drops the pizza as Jesus waves to Jim.

ALEX: Shit!
JIM: Jesus!
MANNY: Jim, no need to yell.
JANET: *(To Tyrone.)* Is that a gun?
TYRONE: *(Quickly hides the gun.)* No.
MARGIE: Brother, hand it over. Now! *(Tyrone gives her the gun. Alex picks up the pizza and walks over to Don. Actor Three crosses to Martha and hands her his sheet music.)*

Note: The following exchanges proceed at a very fast pace. Jim is the only person who sees Jesus.

JIM: *(To Jesus.)* Are you auditioning?

JANET: *(To Jim.)* That's my job.

ACTOR THREE: Yes I am.

TYRONE: *(To Margie, referring to the gun.)* I want that back on my way out.

ALEX: *(To Don.)* Fourteen dollars.

DON: Let me grab my wallet. *(Don reaches for pizza box but Alex holds on tight.)*

ALEX: Cash first! *(Don searches his pockets for his wallet.)*

JIM: *(Trying to point Jesus out to Janet.)* Jesus!

TYRONE: *(To Janet.)* Am I done yet?

JANET: *(To Tyrone.)* No! *(To Jim.)* What's wrong with you?

JIM: Nothing.

JANET: *(To Actor Three.)* Can you ask Santa Claus to wait out in the lobby?

ACTOR THREE: I could.

TYRONE: What about me? *(Monica enters.)*

MONICA: Did everyone forget I was in the lobby? *(Janet, Manny and Don react.)*

JIM: Mom! Oh man, I forgot all about you!

MONICA: The words every mother dreams of hearing from her son.

DON: *(To Alex.)* It's in my coat pocket, hold on.

ALEX: *(To Don as he exits.)* Dude, I'm doubled parked!

MANNY: I thought you were sending her home, Jim.

JIM: *(To Jesus.)* Sorry.

JANET: You should be.

JIM: *(To Janet.)* I was talking to Jesus.

JANET: What? *(Two actors, Gerald and Steve, enter with the numbers eleven and twelve respectively pinned on their shirts. Steve notices the Pizza.)*

STEVE: You people are eating?

GERALD: We've been waiting over an hour to audition!

MARGIE: No one's eating!

ALEX: *(To Margie.)* Whatever!

STEVE: *(Pointing towards the pizza.)* What's that?

JANET: All actors back to the lobby!

(Ted enters dressed like a plumber.)

MARGIE: Who the hell are you?

TED: The plumber, I've come to fix the sink.

TYRONE: *(To Margie.)* Sister, give a brother a break! *(Actor Three sits at the piano starts to play White Christmas. Everyone stops and looks at him.)*

ACTOR THREE: *(Singing.)* I'm dreaming of a white Christmas… *(Tyrone quickly crosses to the piano, grabs the sheet music and rips it up.)*

TYRONE: Oh no you ain't!

ACTOR THREE: What's wrong with that song? It's a classic.

TYRONE: *(Using finger quotes.)* "White" Christmas?

JIM: *(Pointing at Jesus.)* Janet, look, Jesus Christ!

JESUS: She can't see me Jim.

MONICA: I want to go home now!

TED: Can someone tell me what's leaking?

MANNY: Oh yes, Right this way.

JESUS: Jim.

JIM: Jesus. *(Jim starts to cross to Jesus but is suddenly stopped by Actor three with the Santa Claus Puppet.)*

ALEX: *(To Ted.)* It's a friggin freak show in here.

TED: Auditions? I'm a bit of an actor myself.

MANNY: *(Leading Ted off right.)* Really? Who isn't?

SANTA CLAUS PUPPET: *(To Jim.)* You're a bad boy, forgetting your Mother. Santa sees all.

JIM: No, Jesus sees all.

SANTA CLAUS PUPPET: Coal in your stocking this year.

TYRONE: *(To Actor Three.)* Coal, what kind of racist comment is that?

JESUS: *(To Jim.)* He can't see me Jim.

JIM: *(To Jesus.)* What?

ACTOR THREE: *(Passive, to Tyrone.)* Coal in your stocking's racist?

JESUS: *(To Jim.)* Only you…

TYRONE: *(To Actor Three.)* Fucking right.

ACTOR THREE: Why is that racist?

TYRONE: Because, when a kid is *bad* he gets something *black*.

JESUS: *(To Jim.)* Only you…

SANTA CLAUS PUPPET: That's just, stupid.

TYRONE: Stupid?! *(Tyrone's full attention is now centered on the puppet.)* How about this, because you're a plastic little cracker that's why!

STEVE: Can we get a slice of that pizza?

ALEX: Fourteen dollars gets you the whole pie!

JIM: *(To Steve and Alex.)* Would you both shut the hell up…

MARGIE: Jim!

JIM: I'm sorry Margie, but everyone keeps talking over Jesus!

SANTA CLAUS PUPPET: *(About Tyrone.)* Malcom X started it!

MARGIE: Has everyone gone mad here?!

TYRONE: I would like to do my second monologue about a bigot and a racist Santa doll!

ACTOR THREE: *(Correcting him.)* Ventriloquist dummy.

TYRONE: Who you calling a dummy, bigot!

JANET: *(Cutting him off.)* Santa, in the lobby!

SANTA CLAUS PUPPET: Me?

JIM: Jesus, what did you say?

STEVE: *(To Tyrone.)* Hey brother, you do know this is a gay theatre company?

TYRONE: Say what?

JESUS: No one but you can see or hear me.

MONICA: *(To Jim.)* I want to go home.

JIM: Why is that?

MONICA: Because…

SANTA CLAUS PUPPET: *(To Tyrone.)* Didn't you read the posting?

TYRONE: You mean, all you all, are fags?

JANET: Enough!

ACTOR THREE: *(Passive.)* He's calling *me* a bigot.

MARGIE: *(To Janet as she stands.)* What the hell is going on here? *(A short pause as Monica puts on her glasses and sees Margie for the first time.)*

MONICA: Oh my, it's a darkie!

MARGIE AND TYRONE: A what?!

MONICA: The darkies and fags are taking over the world.

ALEX: *(To Manny.)* What the hell did she say?

DON: *(Imitating the Santa Puppet)* Shoot her, she's the bigot.

JANET: Don!

JIM: *(To Jesus who has moved behind Tyrone.)* Jesus, do something!

TYRONE: *(Thinking Jim is talking to him.)* I'll do something; I'll kick your mother's ass!

MONICA: My what?

TYRONE: Old, wrinkly, cracker ass!

STEVE: Bitch is getting read!

JANET: *(To Santa Puppet.)* Santa! *(To Actor Three.)* I mean you! Go wait in the lobby.

DON: *(Enters with wallet.)* Here you are, fourteen dollars.

MANNY: Jim, get your Mother out of here.

ALEX: *(To Tyrone, provoking.)* You just going to stand there?

TYRONE: *(To Margie.)* I swear to God I will kick his, that puppet's and some old lady ass right now!

JIM: Don't swear to God! *(Martha wakes up and starts to play as Jesus exits.)*

JANET: Martha not now!

ALEX: *(To Don.)* No tip?

DON: *(Handing her a tip.)* Oh right, here you go.

JANET: MARTHA!

ALEX: What are you guys doing here?

DON: Auditions. *(Martha suddenly stops playing.)*

JANET: SANTA!

SANTA CLAUS PUPPET: I know, wait in the lobby!

JANET: Then do it!

SANTA CLAUS PUPPET: *(To Tyrone.)* Later.

TYRONE: Fag.

ACTOR THREE: *(Hurt.)* What did you call me?

TYRONE: What? You deaf?

SANTA CLAUS PUPPET: *(Taking over.)* Dude, don't start shit with me!

TYRONE: *(Directly to the puppet.)* Bring it on, little Santa! *(Actor three slaps Tyrone lightly with Santa puppets hand.)*

TYRONE: Oh no he didn't! *(Tyrone grabs the puppet by the neck as Actor three holds on tight.)*

ALEX: *(Egging them on.)* Puppet fight!!

MARGIE: I don't believe this shit. *(Margie shoots the gun in the air. Alex pulls out a gun and shoots over Margie's head. Everyone stops. Margie looks at Alex.)*

ALEX: Oh that's right bitch. Pizza delivery. I'm packing! *(Monica starts to have an attack.)*

MONICA: Fag, fag, fag, darkie, darkie, TRUMP, TRUMP, Lock her up, darkie fuck, shit! (pause) MERRY FUCKING CHRISTMAS! *(Monica passes out on the floor. There is a moment of silence.)*

ALEX: What the hell was that?

JANET: Ten minutes everyone. *(They all start to exit.)*

JANET: *(To Margie.)* She has Tourette's.

MANNY: She's also narcoleptic.

DON: *(To Alex.)* You ever been in a play? *(They all exit. Monica is alone on the floor center stage. Stage lights dim leaving Monica in a special. "The Twister" from The Wizard Of OZ underscores the following voiceover.)*

ACTOR THREE: *(Voiceover.)* What's wrong with that song? It's a classic.

TYRONE: *(Voiceover.)* "White" Christmas?

SANTA CLAUS PUPPET: *(Voiceover.)* You're a bad boy, forgetting your Mother. Santa sees all.

JIM: *(Voiceover.)* No, Jesus sees all.
ALEX: *(Voiceover.)* Fourteen dollars gets you the whole pie!
STEVE: *(Voiceover.)* Hey brother, you do know this is a gay theatre company?
TYRONE: *(Voiceover.)* Old, wrinkly, cracker ass!
MONICA: *(Voiceover.)* Oh my, it's a darkie!
MARGIE: *(Voiceover.)* I don't believe this shit.

Suddenly a loud gun shot then "Feliz Navidad" begins to play as Jesus descends from the heavens in a glass bubble, resembling Glinda the good witch. He is all sparkle and glitter with a flashy Mexican shawl. Monica wakes up. She gets up on her feet. Music stops as Jesus steps onto the stage.

MONICA: Jesus?
JESUS: *(Correcting her with the Hispanic pronunciation.)* It's Jesús.
MONICA: You're a beaner?
JESUS: That's right girl!
MONICA: And a fag?
JESUS: Surprise!
MONICA: Oh God, no!
JESUS: Oh Mary, yes!
MONICA: You can't be gay!
JESUS: Oh yes, I am!
MONICA: No! No!
JESUS: Oh poor thing, you didn't expect *that* did you!
MONICA: I don't believe it! A gay beaner. I need some water. *(Jesus hands Monica the coffee cup from the director's table. Monica takes a sip and spits it out.)* That's wine!
JESUS: *(Laughs.)* Mira. It's an old trick of mine.
MONICA: I'm on medicine!
JESUS: Oh lighten up!
MONICA: Why are you here?
JESUS: Amore.
MONICA: Love? You're looking for a date?
JESUS: No, silly, Para apreciar… to recognize love and devotion between two people of the same sex and other orange shit.
MONICA: Orange...wait... You're not supposed to believe in same sex marriage.
JESUS: Who told you that?
MONICA: The Bible!
JESUS: Oh, the Bible, *(Fists to Heaven.)* Aquele texto podrido e atrasado. Los apostoles, rios en los siglos de confusión... *(To Monica.)* This all started with the deletion of the acento above my name.
MONICA: What?!
JESUS: Two thousand years of "Jesus did this" and "Jesus said that." *(To Audience.)* It's Jesús bitches!
MONICA: This is crazy.
JESUS: Tell me about it girl, weak people in search of more power building walls...etc..etc
MONICA: I must be dreaming, there is no way Jesus is gay. I need a drink. *(Monica takes a sip of the wine spits it out.)* It's water!
JESUS: Got you again!
MONICA: I don't believe this!
JESUS: Let go of your walker!
MONICA: What?

JESUS: I am the Lord, Jesús Christo. You are healed! Walk to me! *(Monica slowly lets go of her walker, takes a step forward, and falls to the floor.)* Oh my, you are so gullible.
MONICA: Why are you doing this to me?
JESUS: It's Christmas! *(Hip Hop dance.)* It's my birthday, it's my birthday. *(Cabbage patch dance.)* Who's your savior, who's your savior? *(Jesus stands center stage. As a bright light starts to shine down on him, he speaks.)* Christmas is a time of forgiveness and love. A time to rejoice! *(A loud crash of thunder)* In light of societal attitudes toward immigrants, women and for all the fucking *(pronounced fooking)* idiots who voted TRUMP! I HAVE RETURNED! *(A loud crash of thunder with a flash of lighting Jesus disappears)*

SNAP TO BLACKOUT.

When lights fade up Monica is still on the floor slowly waking up. Manny, Margie, Janet, Don, Alex and a few actors are standing over her.

MONICA: Jesus can't hate Trump. He can't, he can't.
MANNY: Monica, are you all right?
MONICA: I saw Jesus.
MANNY: What?
MONICA: I mean, Jesús. And it was dark ...then lightning, and he was telling me something, *(Points to Don.)* and you were there, *(To Manny.)* and you, *(To Janet.)* and you, *(To Margie.)* and you darkie...*(Manny helps Monica stand)*
MARGIE: You starting that shit again? *(Jim enters.)*
JIM: What happened?
DON: She had one of her fits.
(Monica starts to exit assisted by Jim.)
MONICA: I saw Jesús.
JIM: Mom.
MONICA: Jimmy, Jimmy, I saw Jesús.
JIM: Who?
MONICA: Jesus!
JIM: Mom, you too!
MONICA: Wait a minute.... JESUS IS A LATINO FAG!
ROD: *(Speaking from off stage right.)* Who's using that word! *(They all stare in horror as Rod enters from stage right with crutches. He has an ace bandage wrapped around his head.)*
MONICA: *(Voiceover.)* JESUS IS A LATINO...
JESUS: *(Voiceover.)* Goddamit! It's Jesús! (loud crash of Thunder)
ALEX: Dude, watch out that light's gonn'a fall on your head.
ROD: *(Rod looks up, then to the audience, and speaks calmly.)* Oh shit.

SNAP TO BLACKOUT.

SOUNDS OF CRASHING LIGHTS.

END OF ACT 1.

ACT 2
SCENE 1

As lights fade up, the "Stable" set is now on stage, including hay, a large star, and maybe a few fake plastic animals. Far stage right a black drape hangs to create the "wings" of the stage. Actors will use this when watching the pageant and will be assumed not seen by the audience. All actors, except Joseph, are sitting around on bails of hay. No one is talking; they are texting on their cell phones. Jim is hammering a few last nails into the manger. Martha is asleep at the keyboard, now placed stage right. After a moment, Janet enters with Margie.

NOTE: Very few stage lights should be used in the following scene to give it more of a "rehearsal" look and feel.

JANET: *(Very loud.)* PLACES! *(Martha wakes with a loud scream and a fart.)*

MARGIE: *(To Janet.)* Ouch, girl, inside voice.

JANET: *(Softer.)* Sorry. Sorry, Martha.

MARTHA: I think I shit myself.

MARGIE: And so it begins.

JANET: All actors need to be in places. And all cell phones should be turned off and put away! No texting during rehearsal! *(Actors move across the stage into their respective places. Jim continues to bang nails into the manger. Manny, Don and Rod enter. Rod is still with one crutch, ace bandage, and holding the shitting Santa. They cross to sit in three empty chairs stage right, next to Martha.)*

MANNY: *(To Rod.)* Sit right there, so you can watch the rehearsal. *(Rod and Margie almost bump into each other, and then give each other a glare. After a pause, Margie exits.)*

ROD: Did you tell her?

MANNY: Not yet.

ROD: You promised me!

MANNY: I'll talk to her.

ROD: When?

MANNY: After!

ROD: The deal was if she continues directing the Shitting Santa makes an appearance.

DON: I'm going to grab a soda. You guys want one?

MANNY: Sounds good.

ROD: Diet please.

DON: Diet it is.

ROD: No caffeine.

DON: No caffeine.

ROD: I like it ice cold.

DON: I'll do my best. *(Don Exits as Manny and Rod sit.)*

ROD: *(Referring to Martha.)* Wonderful. Seats next to the gas tank. *(Tina enters.)*

TINA: Are we supposed to be in costume?

JANET: No costumes.

TINA: Someone better tell Fromage. *(Loud bang from Jim.)*

JANET: *(To Jim.)* Jim, do you have to do that right now?

JIM: Yes, I do. *(Jim continues hammering. Spike enters in full Joseph costume.)*

NOTE: Spike is very effeminate. When entering he should be grooming, and maybe twirl in his new costume as if wearing a formal gown.

JANET: No costumes, Fromage.
SPIKE: *(Deadpan.)* What?
JANET: No costumes.
SPIKE: A little late with *that* announcement.
JANET: You have a few minutes. Take it off.
SPIKE: If only I can find a man to say that to me.
JIM: Take it off.
SPIKE: *(To Jim.)* Oh please Mary, I said a man. *(Spike exits. Margie enters. Another bang from Jim, he has moved to the stable.)*
MARGIE: What are you building Jim, a fort?
JIM: Just making sure *nothing* falls on *anybody's* head. *(Rod moans.)*
JANET: If you built it right the first time…
JIM: If *people* would tend to their own business…
JANET: *(Continuing.)* …*people* wouldn't be in stitches and crutches! *(Rod moans again.)*
JANET: *(To Rod.)* Sorry honey.
JIM: Did you just call me honey?
JANET: You wish.
MARGIE: *(Interrupting.)* Why don't you two just get a room. *(Jim and Janet give Margie a cold stare.)* Wow, can you all feel that sexual tension? *(Actors laugh as Janet pulls Margie down stage right.)*
JANET: *(To Margie.)* what are you doing?
MARGIE: Oh please.
JANET: Please what?
MARGIE: Girl, I see what's going on here.
JANET: I assure you nothing is *going on*.
MARGIE: Oh really?
JANET: Yes, really!
MARGIE: Then why do you keep checking out his ass? *(Janet opens her mouth to speak, but nothing comes out, Margie smiles then moves center to speak with the cast.)* Ok, everyone, *(Margie claps her hands and all actors enter.)* tonight let's try to get through this without stopping. Tomorrow night we're going through our cue-to-cue. *(Shepherd One raises his hand as Janet gets her notebook and sits stage left.)* Yes, Mr. Shepherd?
SHEPHERD ONE: What exactly is a cue-to-cue?
MARGIE: Oh right, sorry, for you actors that have never, well, acted or been on stage before, a cue-to-cue is a rehearsal in which technical issues take precedence over musical and acting issues.
SHEPHERD ONE: Meaning?
JANET: Meaning, large bodies of action or inaction will be omitted as the rehearsal proceeds among the key cues for lighting and set changes.
JIM: There's only *one* set. *(Jim exits.)*
SHEPHERD ONE: *(To Janet.)* Huh?
MARGIE: You will only be doing lines and blocking immediately before and after each scene.
SHEPHERD TWO: We're doing that tonight?
JANET: No, tonight's a full run, tomorrow night we will have the lighting cue-to-cue, in which each lighting change is run.
JIM: *(From off stage.)* We're changing the lights?

JANET: No, we are not changing the lights. *(Jim enters.)*

JIM: I'm not changing lights after I set them at load-in.

JANET: We are not changing lights!

SHEPHERD ONE: Then why do we need to cue them?

SHEPHERD TWO: What's load-in?

WISE MAN ONE: *(To Tina.)* I wish someone knew what was happening around here.

JANET: I wish actors would pay attention.

MARGIE: All right! *(Takes a deep breath.)* Let's begin before we kill each other.

JANET: PLACES! *(Martha squeals and farts.)*

MARGIE: *(To Janet.)* My God girl! We're all right here. Inside voice.

JANET: Sorry.

Actors start to take their places. Ted, the narrator, enters still in his plumber uniform stands stage left. Tina, Innkeeper and Alex walk off stage left, the two shepherds and three wise men go off stage right. Margie sits on a chair placed house left with Janet on her right.

JANET: And, lights up!

SHEPHERD ONE: *(Re-enters confused.)* So, are we doing lights now?

JANET: No!

SHEPHERD ONE: Well, you said lights up.

JANET: That's a cue for us to begin.

SHEPHERD ONE: Why don't you just say, let's begin? *(Jim enters.)*

JIM: You *want* lights now?

JANET: NO! *(Jim exits as several actors step back on stage. Tina enters.)*

TINA: I thought the cue-to-cue was tomorrow.

JANET: It is! Will you all get backstage and let us begin, please. *(All actors exit.)*

MARGIE: *(To Janet.)* Have you ever?

JANET: No. It's like herding cats. *(Spike enters and stands center stage.)*

MARGIE: *(To Spike.)* Hello?

SPIKE: Hello.

JANET: What are you doing?

SPIKE: Are we starting?

JANET: I called places.

SPIKE: Sorry. I was in the dressing room getting out of costume, as I was told to do. *(Spike exits stage left, then re enters and skips to stage right.)*

JANET: *(To Ted.)* Please, begin before anything else happens.

TED: Oh sure. *(Ted opens the book and begins to read. He has an overly strong lisp, so every "S" is exaggerated.)* About two thousand years ago…

JANET: Hold on! What is that?

TED: My lines.

JANET: No, the lisp?

TED: Oh, it's a gay pageant so I thought…

JANET: Don't.

TED: Ok. *(Ted opens the book and begins to read.)* About two thousand years ago…

JANET: Why are you stopping?

TED: There's supposed to be music underscoring this.

JANET: Oh right, sorry.

ROD: *(To Manny.)* This is a nightmare.

JANET: *(Loudly at Martha.)* Martha!

MARTHA: *(Waking up.)* What? What is it, what happened?

JANET: We've started the rehearsal.

ARTHA: What?

JANET: *(Louder.)* We've started the rehearsal!

MARTHA: Oh, my. Why are you shouting!

JANET: I'm sorry, we're starting.

MARTHA: Well, it would be nice if someone informed me.

JANET: Ok, let's start from the beginning. *(Martha starts playing "Oh Little Town of Bethlehem." Jim enters.)*

JIM: You want the light cues this time?

JANET: NO!

JIM: Alright, no need to yell.

MARGIE: Thank you Jim. *(Jim exits.)*

JANET: *(To Ted.)* Continue.

TED: From where I was?

JANET: *(Holding her head in her hands.)* I don't care.

TED: About two thousand years ago, in the town of Nazareth, there lived a young woman named Mary. *(Tina enters.)* She was engaged to be married to Joseph, *(Spike enters.)* a carpenter. *(Spike holds up a hammer.)*

ROD: STOP! *(Martha screams and stops playing. Her sheet music falls to the ground unnoticed.)*

JANET: Rod, what is it?

ROD: *(Rod points to the hammer.)* That! What is that?!

JANET: Fromage.

SPIKE: Yeah?

JANET: What is that?

SPIKE: A hammer.

JANET: I can see it's a hammer, but why is it in your hand?

SPIKE: I thought it was a good idea… you know… carpenter.

JANET: Get rid of it. *(Spike throws the hammer off stage. It hits Alex.)*

ALEX: *(From off stage, loudly.)* Ouch! What the hell was that?

SPIKE: *(To Alex.)* I'm sorry. You ok?

ALEX: *(From off stage.)* You could have killed me! *(Alex enters limping. She has angel wings on but she is dressed very masculine.)*

SPIKE: I'm sorry.

ALEX: Are you insane?

SPIKE: No, Janet told me to.

JANET: What?!

ALEX: *(To Janet.)* Why the hell did you tell him to throw a hammer at me?

JANET: I didn't.

MARGIE: *(To Alex.)* You ok?

ALEX: I guess. *(To Spike.)* You're lucky it landed on my foot and not my head.

MARGIE: Can we continue?

ALEX: Yeah. *(Alex stops and turns towards Janet.)* I don't believe you Janet.

JANET: I didn't tell him to throw it at you!

ALEX: Whatever.

MARGIE: Moving on!

TED: From where?

MARGIE: From where you were.
TED: *(With attitude.)* Ok… *(Ted continues as Martha plays.)* One day an angel appeared before her… *(Alex enters limping while giving Janet a cold stare.)* and told her…
ALEX: *(Pissed off.)* Mary, you have been chosen to have a special baby.
TINA: *(Over acting.)* Really?
ALEX: Yes, the baby will be God's son, and you must call him Jesus. *(Alex exits.)*
TED: Soon after the Angel's visit, Mary and Joseph were married. *(Tina and Spike kiss.)*
SPIKE: *(To Tina.)* Girl, who you been with?
TINA: *(Confused.)* What?
SPIKE: I'm telling you one thing bitch, I better be that baby's daddy.
ROD AND JANET: STOP! *(Martha screams.)*
ROD: I didn't write that!
JANET: *(To Rod.)* Relax honey, I got it. *(To Spike.)* Spike!
SPIKE: *(Correcting her.)* It's Fromage!
JANET: Fromage!
SPIKE: Yeah?
JANET: What was that?
SPIKE: Oh, *(Spike smiles.)* I added a few lines, and blocking. *(To Rod.)* You're welcome.
ROD: What?!
SPIKE: Yeah. I mean, come on, if a straight guy comes home and his *(makes air quotes)* "virgin wife" tells him she's pregnant… I mean, really… He's not gonna buy that whole immaculate inception crap.
ROD: It's *con*ception, and you're fired!
SPIKE: What?
JANET: Relax, Rod, I can handle this. Fromage!
SPIKE: Yeah?
JANET: No ad libbing
SPIKE: I wasn't.
JANET: Just stick to the script!
SPIKE: Ok. *(Spike mumbles to Tina.)* No one's going to buy this crap.
JANET AND ROD: *(Janet to Spike.)* What did you say? *(Rod to Manny.)* What did he say?
SPIKE: I said no one's going to buy this crap!
SHEPHERD ONE: *(Shepherd One pokes his head on stage.)* No one would believe *you* knocked her up either. *(Actors backstage laugh.)*
MARGIE: Moving on! PLEASE!
TED: Mary was due to have her baby… *(Tina, realizing she forgot the pillow, grabs the baby Jesus from the manger and stuffs him under her shirt.)* …when they were told they had to go on a long journey to Bethlehem. *(Martha starts to play "Over the river and thru the woods to grandmother's house we go." From off stage the cast is singing "Oh Little Town of Bethlehem" as Tina and Spike dance looking confused.)*
JANET AND ROD: Stop! *(Martha stops, screams, farts. The Innkeeper enters.)*
Innkeeper: We can't hear a thing back here.
JANET: *(To Rod.)* I got this honey, you just relax.
ROD: *(To Manny about Tina and Spike.)* Fred and Ginger have completely lost control.
MANNY: It'll be fine.
ROD: Easy for you to say, your name's not under playwright.
JANET: Are the backstage monitors on for the cast? *(There is a loud speaker feedback squeal. The entire cast reacts.)*
JIM: *(Jim enters.)* They're on now. *(Jim exits.)*

JANET: Martha, what are you playing?

MARTHA: Hell if I know. *(Don enters with three cans of soda and joins Manny and Rod. Janet walks over to Martha, takes the sheet music and replaces it with "Oh Little Town of Bethlehem.")*

JANET: *This* is what you should be playing.

MARTHA: Now you tell me.

DON: *(To Rod.)* How's it going?

ROD: Don't ask.

JANET: Let's continue.

JIM: *(Jim enters.)* Want lights this time?

JANET: NO!

JIM: Try laying off the…

ROD: *(Noticing the can.)* Caffeine!

DON: It's all they had. *(To Manny, sarcastically.)* Running smooth, huh?

JANET: MOVING ON!

MARGIE: Shit!

JANET: Sorry!

JIM: I'll be in the back alley if anyone needs me!

JANET: We won't.

ROD: *(Stands up.)* Moving on! *(Everyone stares at Rod and he sits quickly. Jim exits.)*

TED: *(Continuing.)* Mary had to ride on a donkey for a few days over the hills of Galilee. *(Martha is playing while the cast sings "Oh Little Town of Bethlehem" off stage. A very bad replica of a donkey appears from stage left, and Tina fakes sitting on it as she and Spike walk back stage right.)*

MARGIE: *(To Janet.)* That's a donkey?

JANET: Talk to Jim.

MARGIE: I will. Make a note.

TED: At last, Mary and Joseph arrived in Bethlehem. *(Tina and Spike get rid of the donkey.)*

ROD: Thank God.

TED: Mary was very tired and needed a place to stay.

TINA: *(Over-acting. As she speaks Joseph's lips move, almost saying her lines.)* I'm very tired, and I need a place to stay.

ROD: *(To Manny.)* She's brilliant.

TED: At each inn, the story was the same. There was no room for them. *(Hand painted signs stick out from stage right and left reading "No Room For Them.")*

MARGIE: What the hell?

JANET: Jim.

MARGIE: Make a note.

TED: Eventually, *(Innkeeper enters stage right.)* one kind Innkeeper said…

Innkeeper: *(Speaking in broken English, very bad acting. Joseph moves his lips almost saying his lines.)* I have no room, but I do have a stable where I keep my animals. You are welcome to stay there. *(Innkeeper exits abruptly. Tina and Spike go into the stable.)*

TED: And so it was that a few hours later, Mary gave birth to her son in that stable. *(A baby falls from between Tina's legs. Spike screams like a girl. Tina acts surprised and picks it up. Spike grabs the baby Jesus and cuddles him.)*

JANET: That's just wrong.

MARGIE: *(To Janet.)* Make a note.

TED: She wrapped Jesus in strips of cloth, *(Spike wraps the baby in rags.)* and laid him in a manger full of hay. *(Tina tries unsuccessfully to get the baby from Spike as he places the baby in the manger.)* Out in the fields overlooking Bethlehem, some shepherds were tending their flocks of sheep by night, *(Shepherds enter.)* when suddenly, a bright light appeared in the sky.

SHEPHERD ONE: *(Waits impatiently for the light, when it does not turn on, looks at Janet.)* Are we doing that?

JANET: No lights.

SHEPHERD TWO: You cut the bright light?

JANET: Just for *this* rehearsal, no lights.

SHEPHERD ONE: It's hard to react without a bright light, Janet.

JANET: Just pretend the light is there.

SHEPHERD ONE: How?

ROD: *(Stands.)* It's called acting! *(Everyone looks at Rod as he sits back down.)*

MARGIE: Continue please.

TED: They were so afraid. *(The shepherds hold each other in fear.)*

ROD: *(To Manny.)* That's so gay.

TED: It was an angel sent by an angel of the Lord. *(Alex enters, still pissed off and limping, and stands on a box behind the shepherds.)* Appearing to the shepherds, the Angel announced...

ALEX: *(Still pissed, delivers the lines very angrily.)* Do not be afraid, for behold, I bring you good tidings of great joy, which will be to all people. For there is born to you this day in the city of David, a Savior, who is Christ the Lord.

ROD: *(To Margie.)* Is that how's she's going to deliver that line?

MARGIE: *(To Alex.)* Can we please focus?

ALEX: Sure, sorry. *(To Janet.)* It's just that I'm still in a little pain. *(Alex repeats her line, this time in a strange angelic character voice.)* Do not be afraid, for behold, I bring you good tidings of great joy, which will be to all people. For there is born to you this day in the city of David, a Savior, who is Christ the Lord.

TED: Suddenly, a great host of heavenly beings appeared with the angels and began singing praises to God. *(A few garlands of angles are dropped to the stage as Martha plays "Angels we have heard on high.")* As the angelic beings departed... *(Alex loses her balance and falls off the box. She screams and lands off stage with a loud crash. Everyone, excluding Martha, Ted and Rod, run over to help her.)*

MARGIE: *(To Alex.)* Are you alright?

ALEX: I quit!

MANNY: You can't quit. We open in two days!

JANET: *(To Spike.)* Get her some water.

SPIKE: Why me?

JANET: You threw the hammer at her!

SPIKE: You told me to! *(Spike exits stage right.)*

MANNY: Let's help her up.

TINA: I don't think you should move her.

SHEPHERD ONE: I'll call 9-1-1. *(Shepherd One removes a cell phone from his pocket.)*

MARGIE: Don't call 9-1-1, she's fine. *(All actors exit except Janet.)*

JANET: *(Turning abruptly to Shepherd One.)* You have a cell phone on during rehearsal?

SHEPHERD ONE: In case of emergencies. *(Janet gives him a cold glare then exits. Shepherd One sits and starts to text on his phone.)*

TED: *(Continuing.)* ...the angel and the shepherds decided to travel to Bethlehem and see the Christ child. *(Most actors start to return to the stage. Looking confused they look at Rod for an answer.)*

TED: After their visit, they began to spread the word about this amazing child and everything. When they arrived at the stable, they were filled with joy at seeing Jesus lying in the manger. They knelt down and worshipped Him. *(Martha starts to play "Angels we have heard on high." This upsets Ted who* *begins to speak louder. All actors look on.)* They told Mary and Joseph how the angel had appeared in the sky and told them that Jesus was to be the Savior of the world. Far away in the East, Wise Men saw a new star shining high in the sky. *(Tyrone enters, slaps the top of the podium and points to Ted, who stops immediately. Martha continues playing.)*

TYRONE: *(to Rod)* I'm here to get my gun!

ROD: *(Rod stands up Martha stops playing.)* You have a gun?

TYRONE: Yes!

ROD: *(Screams.)* Run! He's got a gun!

All actors panic. Ted and Rod run off stage left, actors scatter, Martha stops playing, looks at Tyrone, raises her hands to surrender and farts.

SNAP TO BLACKOUT.

END OF SCENE 1.

ACT 2
SCENE 2

Lights fade up far stage right, on the "Back Alley." Jim is sitting on boxes. Behind them are a few trash cans. He just finished a joint as Tarquin enters. Center stage is dimly lit. Tyrone and Margie have a short conversation then Margie exits. Tyrone follows her.

JIM: Hey.

TARQUIN: Hello.

JIM: You're back?

TARQUIN: Yes, they apologized, as it should be. How's it going?

JIM: Horrible.

TARQUIN: I figured as much. How do they ever get a show up and running? *(Tyrone enters.)*

JIM: May I help you?

TYRONE: Chill out, gay boy. Sister's just retrieving my… personal property.

JIM: I'm straight.

TYRONE: Then I'm white. *(Don enters.)*

DON: *(To Tyrone.)* May I help you?

TYRONE: What the hell's the matter with you white people, can't a brother sit and wait for something without all y'all asking twenty questions? *(Margie enters.)* Sister, can you please hurry. It's getting awful bright up in here.

MARGIE: Just hold on little brother, I put your gun in the safe. Don, you got the key to the safe?

DON: I gave it to Manny. (texting)

MARGIE: *(To Tyrone.)* I'll be right back, and if that gun was loaded when you brought it in, it won't be when you take it out. Why you carry a gun around in the first place? Giving black men a bad rap.

TYRONE: Sister, I'm a black man in a white world, what else do you need to know? *(Margie shakes her head exits. Don continues texting.)*

DON: They're starting rehearsal again in twenty minutes. We should go in.

JIM: Why bother? How's the butch angel?

DON: She'll be ok. You *both* need to be in there when they begin.

JIM: They don't need *me* till tomorrow.

TARQUIN: They don't *need* me at all. The costumes are finished.

DON: I was meaning to ask you about that.

TARQUIN: What?

DON: *(looking up from phone)* Did you change the costumes when we changed the play?

TARQUIN: I added the cowboy costumes!

DON: Is that a yes?

TARQUIN: What?

DON: Look, just make sure they're not over the top, like last play. *(back to texting)*

TARQUIN: And the *play* wasn't? *(Manny enters.)*

MANNY: *(To Tyrone.)* May I help you?

TYRONE: No.

MANNY: *(To Don, Jim and Tarquin.)* What's up?

JIM: Taking a break.

MANNY: They'll be starting in twenty.

TARQUIN: We heard.

MANNY: *(To Don.)* Rod's not happy.

DON: Understood.

MANNY: I bet this will be our last Christmas pageant.

TYRONE: Why are you doing a Christmas pageant anyway?

MANNY: Excuse me?

TYRONE: Isn't this a queer theatre?

MANNY: Yeah.

TYRONE: *(Comparing using hands.)* Queer, Christian. The two together aren't exactly copasetic.

MANNY: There are gay Christians.

TARQUIN: Oh please, in the Christian world there *are* no gay people. We are all just straight people making choices, and sinning.

MANNY: I'm Catholic.

DON: Aren't Catholics Christians?

MANNY: Yeah.

TARQUIN: In the Catholic's realm there are only non-practicing homosexuals.

MANNY: I still go to Mass.

JIM: How's that work out for you?

MANNY: Well, some of our congregation doesn't mind.

TARQUIN: And the other ninety-nine percent?

MANNY: I ignore.

DON: *(still texting)* How did we ever get this conversation started? *(looks directly at Tyrone.)* Oh, yeah.

TYRONE: What? I asked a question. I can't do that? Ask a question?

DON: *(texting as he continues)* It's the *way* you ask. So militant, like most…

TYRONE: Like most what? Nig…

DON: *(Quickly interrupting.)* I was not going to use that word.

TYRONE: I bet you thought it. Mother fucking texting asshole.

DON: Really?

TYRONE: (same inflection) Yeah really.

DON: It's not your business.

TYRONE: It's disrespectful, that's what it is, disrespectful, never even looks anyone in the eye, carries his little phone everywhere, texting all his white privileged friends.

DON: What pissed you off the most: that I have friends or a phone?

TYRONE: Neither, it's your shitty privileged attitude.

DON: Says the militant gun carrying black man.

TYRONE: Militant? Know what, everything you think you know about black men, you have been misinformed.

DON: And everything you think you know about gay men…

TYRONE: I don't know shit about gay men. I don't need to know shit about them.

DON: Ignorance is bliss.

TYRONE: Faggot, why are you talking to me?

DON: Why is it I can't use the "N" word but you can call me faggot.

TYRONE: Because bitch, you don't have that right!

DON: Okay, so I'm a bitch now?

TYRONE: A big bitch.

DON: Stay ignorant, it suits you.

TYRONE: You have any questions white boy?

TARQUIN: I have a question. Why do black people walk so slow when you're crossing the street?

TYRONE: What the hell *are* you?

MANNY: *(Interrupting.)* Gentleman! *(Pauses.)* Did I ever tell you about my childhood?

TYRONE: I'll be leaving soon. Just tend to your own affairs.

MANNY: *(Continuing.)* Well, when I was a kid, in Mexico, my parents and I used to attend a small, impoverished, Catholic Church, just outside Hermosillo.

JIM: I've heard of that city.

TARQUIN: That's where he buys his pot.

MANNY: Actually, Hermosillo is known as the City of the Oranges, because of the abundance of oranges in its territory. *(Lights fade up dimly on the stable, which has converted into a small church. Actors enter with shawls over their heads, looking like parishioners. They all have an orange in their hands, some are eating them.)*

MANNY: *(Continuing.)* The church was located just outside the city. I loved that church, nothing fancy. What I remember most is Christmas. That's when that little building turned magical for me. Walking to that small church Christmas morning, *(The cast on stage begin to sing "De Colores" softly.)* hearing the parishioners singing De Colores, that beautiful sound filling the air. My parents and me, hand in hand, filled with the spirit of Christmas. It was on one of those walks, many years later, that I told my parents I was gay. Soon after, my parents confided in our priest. He told them homosexuality, meaning me, was an abomination. It wasn't long till the entire congregation heard of the news. People started making derogatory comments to my parents, and eventually me. But my Mother, being a strong, intelligent, religious woman, told me...

Tina becomes Manny's Mother, Shepherd Two becomes his Father, and they speak with a thick Spanish accent.

TINA: Son, I don't believe God would put you on this Earth to be an "abomination." Being gay is not bad; it's who you are – a loving creation of Dios.

SHEPHERD TWO: There are many people in our faith that will try and convince you otherwise. All I can say is, you must trust yourself, your own feelings, and your own relationship with God.

TINA AND SHEPHERD TWO: We love you, son. *(Singing stops. Lights out on the stable, lights up on the alley.)*

JIM: Wow, oranges.

MANNY: What?

JIM: Like the orange President who wants a wall to keep you out.

TARQUIN: Jim's tripping.

DON: You never told me that story.

MANNY: I did. You were texting.

TYRONE: Huh. *(as if to say to Don see I told you)*

MANNY: Needless to say, my parents and I are still very close.

DON: They still go to that church?

MANNY: Sadly, no. It eventually, progressively, got worse.

TYRONE: After all that shit, and you still attend the Catholic church?

MANNY: I do.

DON: Why?

MANNY: I listen to the Spirit, not the lunatics.

TARQUIN: I wish my story were as nice as that. *My* parents are not that subtle.

DON: Do tell.

TARQUIN: When I told them I was gay they weren't exactly thrilled.

Lights up on the stable, out on the alley. Tina becomes Tarquin's Mother, Shepherd Two becomes his Father, in a small special center stage. Actors stand behind now sporting Yarmulkes in a frozen position with a "Why" expressions on their faces. The song "Hava Nagila" plays softly behind the dialogue.

TINA: *(Very Jewish.)* A Klog is mir.* Vat, are you trying to kill me?
SHEPHERD TWO: *(Very Jewish.)* I'm Fahklumpt, Famisched, Farblondzhet!** *(Lights out on the stable, lights up in the alley.)*
TARQUIN: *(To the men in the alley.)* We're Jewish. *(Lights out on the alley, lights up on the stable.)*
TINA: Vat do you mean you're gay!
SHEPHERD TWO: This boy is Hockin me a chinick.
TINA: *(Cries out.)* My boy likes the Shmeckle!*** *(Lights out on the stable, lights up in the alley. All look to Tarquin for definition, he points to his crotch.)*
TARQUIN: Shmeckle.
JIM/DON/MANNY: *(Almost Jewish, sounding the long "O.")* Oh. *(Music stops.)*
JIM: That's funny, speckled.
TARQUIN: *(Correcting him.)* It's shmeckle.
DON: I think I'll steal that. *(Pause.)*
TARQUIN: *(To Jim.)* So, straight boy…
JIM: What?
TARQUIN: What's your story?
JIM: I have no story, other than I've seen Jesus.
TYRONE: Man, why do you keep saying that?
JIM: Because it's true.
TARQUIN: He smokes a lot of pot.
TYRONE: That's some good shit.
JIM: So, no doubt I believe in him, he's cool actually. But unlike you guys I never had to come out.
TYRONE: You're really straight?
JIM: Yep.
TARQUIN: Do you remember any of your childhood?
JIM: Not much.
DON: It figures, sometimes he forgets what day it is.
TARQUIN: Come on, you must remember something?
JIM: Well, now that I think about it, I do remember a story my Dad told me.
TARQUIN: Go on.
JIM: It's a story from when I was a little baby.

The song "In-A-Gadda-Da-Vida" by Iron Butterfly starts playing. Lights fade up on the stable. All actors are stoners from the sixties. A younger Monica emerges from the group dressed as a hippy. She's holding Jim as a newborn baby wrapped in a blanket in one arm, and a large bong in the other. She tries to light the bong, dropping the baby on its head. Lights out on stable, lights up on the alley. All the guys are horrified.

MANNY: Wow.

* *A Klog is mir = Woe is me.*
** *Fahklumpt = Mixed up. Although this one is more of an emotionally based mixed up-ness. Famisched = Another of the confused series of words. Farblondzhet = Lost, bewildered, confused.*
*** *Shmeckle = Penis*

TYRONE: Harsh.
DON: Sick.
TARQUIN: Yeah, but it explains a lot. *(To Don.)* What about you?
DON: I got nothing.
TARQUIN: I've heard that about you.
DON: Very funny. I meant my parents were atheist so they never went to church.
MANNY: Never?
DON: Never. They went dancing instead, and to happy hour.
TARQUIN: I like them already.
JIM: When did you tell them you were gay?
DON: I didn't.
MANNY: They don't know?
DON: I didn't tell them I was gay, I asked them.
TYRONE: What?
DON: I asked them.
TARQUIN: How old were you?
DON: Ten.
MANNY: What?
DON: It was later that night, after they had a few martinis, that I asked them about my being gay.

Lights up on the stable. Shepherd One and Shepherd Two play Don's parents. They are dressed in 1970's disco outfits, each holding a martini glass. The Village People plays loudly as they shout over the music.

SHEPHERD ONE: Well of course you're gay you silly little thing! That's why we adopted you!
SHEPHERD TWO: You came that way!
SHEPHERD ONE: And don't you listen to that right wing bigot Jerry Falwell. Gay people are not making choices.
SHEPHERD TWO: It's not a choice, it's an orientation!
SHEPHERD ONE: I hear you girl! *(snap)*
SHEPHERD TWO: Right! *(snap)*
SHEPHERD ONE: I mean, come on, doesn't she know Jesus was gay?
SHEPHERD TWO: Surrounded by twelve male apostles, one named *Peter*.
SHEPHERD ONE: Oh honey, stop it!
SHEPHERD TWO: And, he wore a dress.
SHEPHERD ONE: I'm moving away from you before the lightning strikes.
SHEPHERD TWO: Please, can we say sister!
SHEPHERD ONE: Thank you Jesus!
SHEPHERD TWO: Enough of this silly chat. Donny, make daddy another cocktail.
SHEPHERD ONE: And not too much vermouth this time! *(They hold their glasses out as light snaps off them and up on the alley. All but Manny are passing a joint.)*
TYRONE: Wow, dude, that just blew my high.
JIM: Your parents were gay?
DON: Yep.
MANNY: You never told me that.
DON: You never asked.

TARQUIN: I hated the seventies. Too much polyester.

DON: *(To Tyrone.)* Well?

TYRONE: What?

DON: You going to share?

TYRONE: My bad, I didn't mean to bogart the joint. *(Passes the joint to Jim.)*

DON: I meant your story.

TYRONE: No.

MANNY: Come on Tyrone.

TARQUIN: We all shared.

JIM: Your turn.

TYRONE: You really want to hear about my childhood?

MANNY: Yeah.

DON: Why not?

TYRONE: Ok, but my childhood wasn't as nice as yours.

TARQUIN: Do tell.

TYRONE: I was number seven, out of fourteen children.

JIM: Fourteen?

TARQUIN: Your poor mama's vagina.

MANNY: Tarquin!

TARQUIN: What? Fourteen kids!

TYRONE: *(Tyrone speaks in a sad, depressed, but very getto tone.)* We were poor, very poor, so poor, my mother had to find food for us anyway she could. She had no money to go shopping.

Theme from "Shaft" plays. Lights fade up on the stable. Actors are facing up stage, all wearing very large afro wigs. Innkeeper enters in full drag as Tyrone's Mother resembling Pam Grier as Foxy Brown. Her heels are comically high. She has a very large handbag strapped over her shoulder.

TYRONE'S MOTHER: Bitch, God dam, just what am I supposed to do, fourteen kids and only one pussy! *(Tyrone's Mother pulls a dead cat out of her bag. After a moment she calls out.)* Henry! Oh, Henry!

TYRONE'S FATHER: *(Yalling from off stage.)* Yes Liza!

TYRONE'S MOTHER: Did ya fetch the water? *(Actor One enters carrying a bucket with a big hole in it. He looks like a pimp.)*

TYRONE'S FATHER: Go fetch the water? There's a hole in the bucket, dear Liza, dear Liza. There's a hole in the bucket, dear Liza, a hole.

TYRONE'S MOTHER: Well fix it, dear Henry, dear Henry, dear Henry. Well fix it!

TYRONE'S FATHER: With what shall I… *(Suddenly a "record scratch" sounds as Don interrupts. Lights change to the alley.)*

DON: Wait a minute…Wait a minute! That's not your childhood, that's a Harry Belafonte song!

MANNY: That's where I heard it!

TYRONE: *(Laughs.)* You really think I'm going tell you bitches my childhood story. *(Janet enters.)*

JANET: Gentlemen, we're at places.

MANNY: Thanks Janet. *(Everyone but Tyrone exits as Margie enters with the gun.)*

TYRONE: Finally.

MARGIE: Here you go, try not to kill anybody!

TYRONE: Not so fast sister.

MARGIE: What?

TYRONE: Sister, you are fine. Why don't we chill sometime… you… me…bottle of wine..

MARGIE: I'm a lesbian.

TYRONE: Say what? No way… come on, you?

MARGIE: Save it.

TYRONE: All right…all right… *(He takes a MAGA hat out of jacket and puts it on)*

MARGIE: What's that?

TYRONE: What? Oh the hat? Yeah, I voted for him.

MARGIE: *(Very aggressive.)* Brother, move your ass on out of here!

TYRONE: Fine! You're all some weird ass angry people in there.

MARGIE: Pick a side brother.

TYRONE: Looks like I have.

MARGIE: He's tearing this country apart.

TYRONE: No, he's shining a light into the shadows. Goodnight beautiful. *(Tyrone exits quickly. Margie enters the stage where Jim sits at the piano and Janet is reading her notes center stage.)*

MARGIE: Let's get this over with. *(Margie exits. Janet starts to follow her.)*

JIM: Do you need me?

JANET: No.

JIM: I didn't mean you personally.

JANET: I know what you meant. The answer is still no.

JIM: I'll be out here if you change your mind. *(Starts to play the piano)*

JANET: Try to keep yourself on this planet.

JIM: On this planet?

JANET: Don't get high.

JIM: *(Giggles.)* Oops, too late.

JANET: Seriously, keep it under wrap!

JIM: I'll do my best.

JANET: *(Suddenly angry.)* Listen you little shit, this is my one opportunity to work with a professional director to have something legitimate on my resume, so don't you *even* try to mess this up for me! I mean it, stay away from the funny stuff, wacky weed, ganja, Mary Jane, whatever you call it. Because dude, I know you are up against the stem. *(Rod enters, unnoticed by Janet.)*

JIM: Uh, Janet?

JANET: Shut up! Do you think I enjoy this? All this *gay* crap? "Okla-Homo," "The Wizard is Odd," gay show after gay show! I miss normal refined theater. Desperately wanting to do one *normal* show again! You know, when the girl gets the boy, just once. Why does everything have to be so GAY! *(Janet turns and sees Rod. Speechless she covers her mouth.)*

ROD: I had no idea you felt that way Janet.

JANET: I don't… not about you… let me explain.

ROD: No, I get it.

JANET: Rod…

ROD: No, it's fine, I'm glad I now know your true feelings.

JANET: That's not how I feel… I mean…

ROD: Don't think I've never heard those bigoted remarks before.

JANET: I'm not a bigot.

ROD: No?

JANET: No.

ROD: A *normal* play refers to… what?

JANET: Maybe that was a bad word to choose. Rod, I'm tired, it's been a long night, a long process with this pageant.

ROD: I'm beginning to think Manny and I put a lot of trust in the wrong people.

JANET: No, Rod, please, I respect that you trusted me, gave me this opportunity right out of college. But...

ROD: But, *too gay* for you?

JANET: No, it's just... well... I miss the shows we did in college. Neil Simon, Arthur Miller, Shakespeare. Can't we do one straight play? Why does everything have to be gay?

ROD: Because, Janet, it's who we are! We are gay, therefore this is a gay theater!

JANET: I get it, you're gay, but isn't there more to your life than that?

ROD: You would never understand. What would you know of the gay culture? Simply put, we do gay theater, because it's who and what we are, so we can be heard, seen and represented. It's gay people that make theatre fabulous. If you don't like it here Janet, leave, there are about a hundred heterosexual theaters in this city, don't let us hold you down. *(Rod begins to exit)*

JANET: Just hold on a minute Rod! I'm not going to let you dump that shit on me!

ROD: Excuse me, dump what shit on you?

JANET: That I don't understand gay culture.

ROD: Well...your comments...

JANET: Might have been slightly ignorant.

ROD: Slightly?

JANET: Regardless, your response didn't need to be peppard with insults. You're just as ignorant about women's issues.

ROD: Women's issues?

JANET: Yes Rod, women also struggle with equality.

ROD: Oh please...

JANET: See, that's exactly what I'm talking about, you haven't a clue. Do you even have a clue that women's issues were defined as women's struggles for the achievement of equal rights and privileges?

ROD: Since when?

JANET: Since forever...and it'll continue if women are subordinate to men in societies. Let's talk about sexual and reproductive health...

ROD: Let's not...

JANET: Domestic violence, equal pay for equal work, sexual harassment and abuse...

ROD: Janet I...

JANET: Women struggle Rod!

ROD: You've made your point Janet.

JANET: You've missed the point Rod. The fact is, I've noticed you know very little about, or even acknowledge, other people's struggles. You talk endlessly, yell, criticises and refuse to listen. What are you bitching about? You have everything, you're in good health, have the right to marry a devoted husband, security.

ROD: Hiring and Firing.

JANET: Then fire me Rod!

ROD: Uh, no, that's never going to happen. Just keep your struggles to yourself. *(he exits)*

JIM: Janet?

JANET: Shut up. *(pause)* Sorry.

JIM: It's okay.

JANET: He's an arrogant ass.

JIM: Maybe, but wow, I sure learned a lot.

JANET: Like?

JIM: That women and gays have more in common than the obvious. Both have been told for years to shut up. I take for granted a lot of things, the simplest thing in life, fall in love, marry the person you love, without the fear of retribution. Being able to walk down a street alone fearlessly. Making my own decisions with my body...

JANET: A ridiculous argument.

JIM: I assume Rod's life is here. His voice, his world. He creates a place for his community to feel welcome, accepted, maybe that's why he's so passionate about it. And you want...need to be respected, listened to, and simply be treated as an equal, capable adult, who has the right to make her own choices.

JANET: *(Pauses.)* Thank you.

JIM: Welcome.

JANET: I had no idea you were so… smart.

JIM: Was that a compliment?

JANET: It was.

JIM: Wow, a compliment. *(Janet starts to exit.)* Where you going?

JANET: I have to go apologize to Rod.

JIM: *(Snap.)* You go girl...and...wait for yours, he owes you one. *(Janet laughs and starts to exit.)*

JIM: Hey!

JANET: What?

JIM: That was the nicest thing you ever said to me, that I'm smart.

JANET: Well, don't get used to it.

JIM: You actually have a heart.

JANET: You better not tell anybody that or I will kill you.

JIM: *(Pauses.)* Would you be interested in dinner?

JANET: I ate already.

JIM: I meant sometime.

JANET: Sometime might work. *(Don enters.)*

DON: Hey Janet, Margie's looking for you, she wants to begin.

JANET: Thank you Don. Where's Rod? I need to talk to him first.

DON: I think he's back stage beating up a shepherd.

JANET: Thank you. *(Janet stops, turns to Don and gives him a big hug.)* You've always respected women. *(Janet exits.)*

DON: What the hell was that about? *(Jim hugs Don and exits.)* What the hell's going on here?

SNAP TO BLACKOUT.

END OF SCENE 2.

ACT 2
SCENE 3

Lights fade up on Margie, Manny, Don, Jim, and Janet standing stage right. Margie paces as she talks.

MANNY: I can't believe we made it.

JANET: Yes, opening night!

DON: That first rehearsal went so bad.

MARGIE: Wait, you mean tonight is opening night?

DON: Yes.

MARGIE: Wait a minute, no one told *me* that. When do we get a dress rehearsal?

MANNY: Actually, last night *was* dress rehearsal.

MARGIE: What? I didn't see any costumes!

MANNY: I know.

JANET: That's how Tarquin works.

MARGIE: You mean to tell me, you don't get to see the costumes till opening night?

MANNY: It's understood.

MARGIE: I don't believe it.

DON: Nothing to worry about. Tarquin is very creative.

MARGIE: This is shit.

MANNY: *(To Jim.)* Did you find a place for the shitting Santa?

JIM: I placed it on stage in the stable.

MARGIE: What?! That thing is on the stage?

MANNY: It was Rod's only request.

MARGIE: *(To Jim.)* Can you see it from the house?

JIM: No!

MARGIE: Manny, Santa wasn't at the birth of Christ.

DON: Shitting.

MANNY: I know!

JANET: Come on everyone, we have a lot to be thankful for.

DON: True, the show is up. I thought we would have to change the name of the play, again.

MANNY: Rod did that already. We all agreed "The Christmas Pageant" is a great title.

DON: I know it is, but, after that rehearsal, we could've called it "The Gayest Christmas Pageant Ever." *(Everyone stops and looks at Don.)*

MARGIE: Oh my God!

JANET: Holy crap!

MANNY: That's it!

DON: What? What did I say?

MARGIE: That's the title!

DON: What?

MANNY: That could save our ass!

DON: I was kidding.

JANET: Don, you're a genius!

DON: You really think "The Gayest Christmas Pageant Ever" is good?

MARGIE: Good? It's great!

MANNY: Call it what it is.

MARGIE: Call it that, or "Joseph is a Fairy."

DON: It's too late. The programs have been printed.

MANNY: It's only the cover!

MARGIE: Right, reprint the cover!

DON: The house opens in three hours!

JANET: Quick Print down the block…

MANNY: It's open twenty-four hours.

MARGIE: Let's do it!

DON: Wait a minute! I've already sent out all the press releases.

MANNY: No one reads our press releases anymore.

DON: That's true.

JANET: We haven't had a critic in the audience in four years.

DON: Can't say I blame them.

MARGIE: Let's get going, we're killing time!

MANNY: Right! *(They all start to leave.)*

DON: Wait! *(They all stop.)*

MANNY: What is it?

DON: Who's going to pay for this?

MARGIE: I will!

DON: Let's do it! *(They all start to leave.)*

MANNY: Wait!

JANET: What?!

MANNY: That was M&M's play.

MARGIE: Who?

MANNY: M&M, the playwright director we hired. He quit, you took over.

DON: That's where I heard it before.

JANET: Shit!

DON: Wait! He doesn't own the copyright to *that* title.

MANNY: Are you sure?

DON: I read his play. The title was "The Gayest Christmas Pageant," period.

MANNY: No *ever*?

DON: No ever!

JANET: Yahoo!

MANNY: What about Rod?

DON: What about him?

MANNY: We have to consult with him on this.

DON: He'll never go for it.

MANNY: We don't know that yet.

JANET: Never mind, let's just forget about it.

MARGIE: My name is on this!

MANNY: And Rod's isn't?

DON: Rod will never go for it.

MANNY: He will if I speak with him first.

MARGIE: Can we please do something before we open!

JANET: Please!

MANNY: Let's get going before it's too late!

DON: Wait, wait, do you really think people are going to come see a play titled "The Gayest Christmas Pageant Ever."

ALL: *(House lights up as actors look right at the audience.)* Shit! *(House lights out.)*

SNAP TO BLACKOUT.

END OF SCENE 3.

ACT 2
SCENE 4

The stable set is on the stage with one added feature: a large Christmas tree now sits stage left. The scene opens with Martha sitting at the keyboard, wearing a Santa Claus costume and tennis shoes. The tree lights illuminate one string at a time as Martha plays a dramatic version of "Oh Christmas Tree" and actors hum off stage. Soon, strings of Christmas lights are being illuminated on the stable and around the stage, including a curtain of stars upstage. Stage lights fade up as Ted takes his position at the podium placed in front of the tree. Rod and Manny enter just off stage right. This area will be used as the "wings" and will be assumed not seen by the audience.

NOTE: This time warm colorful stage lighting should be used to give a more "live" theatre feel. All actors are in full costume.

ROD: Where's my Santa?

MANNY: It's there.

TED: *(To Manny and Rod.)* Shhhh! *(Manny points stage right where the shitting Santa sits, almost completely covered in hay. Martha begins to play "Oh Little Town Of Bethlehem." As he speaks the lisp has made a return)* About two thousand years ago, in the town of Nazareth, there lived a young woman named Mary. *(Tina enters.)* She was engaged to be married to Joseph, *(Spike enters.)* a carpenter. *(Spike holds up the hammer as Rod moans.)* One day an angel appeared before her *(Alex enters dressed as a very beautiful angel with extremely large wings.)* and told her…

ALEX: *(Speaking in high-pitched voice.)* Mary, you have been chosen to have a special baby.

TINA: *(Over-acting.)* Really?

ALEX: Yes, the baby will be God's son and you must call him Jesus. *(Alex exits stage left making a oooh ahhh sound.)*

TED: Soon after the angel's visit, Mary and Joseph were married. *(Tina and Spike kiss.)*

SPIKE: Mary?

TINA: *(Confused.)* Yeah? *(Rod clears his throat. Spike sees him.)*

SPIKE: Never mind. *(Rod and Manny exit)*

TED: Mary was due to have her baby, *(Tina stands and has a very large belly.)* when they were told they had to go on a long journey to Bethlehem. *(Martha starts to play "Oh Little Town of Bethlehem" as Joseph and Mary sing. Crossing stage right.)*

TINA AND SPIKE: *(Singing.)* Oh little town of Bethlehem, How still we see thy… laid… *(Forgetting the lyrics they look to each other and run off stage right. Rod quickly enters picking up where they left off. As he moves to the stable to retrieve the shitting Santa he trips on a cord causing an electrical spark. He quickly picks up the shitting Santa.)*

ROD: *(Singing, he ends the lyric just as he places the Santa on the tree.)* Above thy deep and dreamless sleep, the silent stars go by.

TED: *(Continues.)* Mary had to ride on a donkey for a few days over the hills of Galilee. *(Tina and Spike re-enter stage left with a toy horse. Tina fakes sitting on it as Spike pulls on the reins they continue to walk back stage right.)*

TED: *(Continues.)* At last Mary and Joseph arrived in Bethlehem. Mary was very tired and needed a place to stay.

MARY: *(Over-acting. As she speaks Spike moves his lips, almost saying her lines.)* I'm very tired. I need a place to stay.

TED: At each inn, the story was the same. There was no room for them. Eventually, one kind innkeeper said… *(Innkeeper enters stage right.)*

Innkeeper: *(Very bad acting. Joseph moves his lips almost speaking his lines.)* I have no room, but I do have a stable where I keep my animals. You are welcome to stay there. *(Innkeeper exits quickly. Mary and Joseph go into the stable.)*

TED: And so it was that a few hours later, Mary gave birth to her son in that stable. *(Mary makes a quick turn upstage then to the audience as the baby Jesus suddenly/magically appears in her arms, Mary acts amazed at the trick.)* She wrapped the Jesus in strips of cloth and laid Him in a manger full of hay. *(Mary follows the directions and places Jesus in cloth then in the manger.)* Out in the fields, overlooking Bethlehem, some shepherds were tending their flocks of sheep by night… *(Shepherds enter, shirtless with cowboy hats, glittery/shiny vests, Daisy Duke shorts and boots/UGGs.)* when suddenly, a bright light appeared in the sky. *(A bright white light shines on them.)* They were so afraid. *(One shepherd jumps into the other's arms and they hold each other.)* It was an angel sent by an angel of the Lord. *(Alex appears behind the shepherds.)* Appearing to the shepherds, the angel announced…

ALEX: *(High-pitched voice.)* Do not be afraid, for behold, I bring you good tidings of great joy which will be to all people. For there is born to you this day in the city of David a Savior, who is Christ the Lord.

TED: Suddenly a great host of heavenly beings appeared with the angels and began singing praises to God. *(A few garlands of angles are dropped to the stage Martha plays and on stage cast sings "Angels We Have Heard On High.")*

CAST: *(Singing. Alex takes over the song, singing loudly.)* Angels we have heard on high, *(Tina and Spike sing with her in harmony.)* Sweetly singing o'er the plains. *(Music stops)*

TED: As the angelic beings departed. *(The Angels depart. Spotlight on the shepherds as they still hold each other, both now standing.)*

SHEPHERD ONE: I wish I knew how to quit you. *(The shepherds kiss, then the music and singing resumes.)*

CAST: *(Singing.)* And the mountains in reply, Echoing their joyous strains.

SPIKE: *(Spike takes over the song imitating Mariah Carey, even putting one finger in his ear like he's trying to find his pitch, at the dismay of other cast members.)* Oh, oh oh, Gloria…

CAST: *(Taking back the song.)* in excelsis Deo! *(The last "Deo" turns into a competition between Tina and Alex to see who can hold the last note longest, with Alex winning in a very annoying high pitch squeal.)*

ALEX: *(To Tina.)* Whatever!

TED: The Angel and the shepherds decided to travel to Bethlehem and see the Christ-child. *(They cross to the stable.)* There they found Mary, Joseph and the baby in the stable. They knelt down and worshipped Him. *(Shepherd One kneels down as Joseph turns his crotch towards him, almost resembling a sex act. Shepherd Two notices and pulls Shepherd One quickly up by the arm, Alex audibly reacts and looks away in disgust, Ted attempts to distract the audience by emphasizing his next line.)* Far, far away in the East, Wise Men saw a new star shining high in the sky. *(The large star begins to shine as three wise men enter. They are dressed way over the top, high comical hats, full colorful tights, long glittery robes. Think Boy George gone wrong.)*

WISE MEN THREE: *(Referring to their costumes.)* Don we now our gay apparel.

TED: These men studied the stars and they knew this was a very special star.

WISE MAN ONE: Wow, isn't that special.

TED: They studied their scrolls *(The Wise Men open a scroll.)* where it said…

WISE MAN TWO: Whenever a bright new star appeared it meant that a great ruler had been born.

WISE MAN THREE: Word.

TED: The Wise Men decided to find this new ruler. They went to Jerusalem to see King Herod. *(Martha plays "We Three Kings" as they travel across the stage quickly. King Herod appears in full leather.)*

WISE MAN ONE: Hey Herod, can we see the child that would be king of the Jews?

TED: The king was troubled.

KING HEROD: I'm troubled.

WISE MAN ONE: And I smell cowhide.

TED: He thought this new king might take away his throne. He told them…

KING HEROD: Return when you have found the baby so that I can worship the child myself.

WISE MAN THREE: *(To Herod.)* That's twisted.

KING HEROD: Remember, see me after you see the baby.

WISE MAN TWO: If we remember, we will.

KING HEROD: I'll beat your ass if you don't. What are your names?

TED: Not wanting to reveal their real names, they offered false ones.

WISE MAN ONE: S.

WISE MAN TWO: N.

WISE MAN THREE: M.

KING HEROD: S-N-M?

TED: *(Pounds the podium.)* And it was then that S&M was born. *(The full cast does a "take" quickly to the audience and then back.)* The Wise Men set off to find the baby. *(As each wise man crosses to stable they sing a verse as Martha plays "We Three Kings.")*

WISE MAN ONE: *(Singing.)* O, star of wonder, star of might.

WISE MAN TWO: *(Singing.)* Star with royal beauty bright.

WISE MAN THREE: *(Singing.)* Westward leading, still proceeding,

ALL CAST: *(Singing.)* Guide us to the perfect light.

TED: The star guided them to the stable in Bethlehem. There they knelt down and worshipped Jesus *(The Wise Men kneel.)* and gave him gifts of gold, frankincense and myrrh. *(The Wise Men give Tina a gold chain that says Jesus, air freshener and a bottle of Polo Black as Ted mentions each of the gifts.)*

TINA: *(To Wise Men.)* What are you doing?

WISE MAN THREE: Giving thanks and praise, *Mary.*

TED: *(Pounds the podium.)* And it was then that "Mary" became part of the gay culture. *(The full cast does a "take" quickly to the audience and then back.)*

WISE MAN ONE: It is right to give this baby thanks and praise.

WISE MAN TWO: For he has come to save the world.

WISE MAN THREE: And soon we will have disorganized religion.

All actors are on stage gathered around the manger. They begin to sing "Away In a Manger." As they sing the manger begins to smoke. Tina is the first to notice. She nudges Spike who makes a loud gasp like a girl. Tina tries to put the small fire out by fanning it with her dress. The smoke continues.

ANGEL: *(Noticing the smoke.)* Holy shit!

(The cast continues to sing the second verse. Suddenly a flame arrears in the smoke, which startles Joseph.)

JOSEPH: Jesus!

(Angel exits, the cast continues to sing and the smoke grows. Soon the entire cast notices.)

SHEPHERD ONE: *(To Shepherd Two.)* Let's go. *(They both exit.)*

TED: *(Looking at the fire.)* What the fuck? *(He exits.)*

WISE MAN ONE: *(Turns upstage and addresses Joseph.)* Do something!

Joseph shakes his head no. Wise Man Two and Wise Man Three exit as Wise Man One tries to pick up the baby Jesus, but finds it really hot. He tosses it to Joseph, who tosses it to Tina. Martha, undaunted, continues playing, and the cast continues singing. When the verse gets to 'asleep in the hay'. Tina tosses the baby back to Joseph, who delivers the final 'hay' when he catches it. Finding it really hot, he tosses it off stage and hits Alex. She enters holding the charred baby upside down by its feet.

ANGEL: What the hell! *(The burnt baby burns her fingers.)* Ouch! Jesus Christ!

Alex drops the baby. Stage lights quickly fade, leaving only the Christmas tree and shitting Santa in a solo light. A Santa "Ho Ho Ho" sound effect is heard, then a loud farting as the shitting Santa eliminates on the tree. The siren of a fire truck is heard in the distance.

FADE TO BLACKOUT.

END OF SCENE 4.

ACT 2
SCENE 5

It is the following morning. Setting is the stable, same as the last scene. When lights fade up, Don enters and sits on a bail of hay. A moment later Jim enters. They look at each other. Don shakes his head "no" and Jim sits. Margie and Janet enter. Margie is carrying a suitcase. She finds her own bail of hay and sits. Janet looks at Jim then to Don.

JANET: *(To Don.)* Anything yet?

DON: Not a word.

MARGIE: How did this happen?

JIM: I think it was the Christmas lights.

MARGIE: What?

JIM: An electrical short in a wire.

MARGIE: I'm talking about the critics!

JIM: Oh.

JANET: Why did you invite them, Don?

DON: I invite them to every show. They never showed up before.

MARGIE: Just my luck, they *show up* opening night.

JIM: I think…

JANET: *(Interrupting.)* No one cares what you think!

JIM: Excuse me?

JANET: This is your fault!

JIM: My fault?

JANET: You built the set!

JIM: Making the critics come?

JANET: Yes, and causing the fire.

JIM: That's crap.

JANET: Crap or not, it happened! *(Manny enters with a L.A. Times in hand. Everyone takes notice.)*

MARGIE: *(Standing.)* Is that it?

JANET: What did they say?

DON: Is it bad?

MANNY: What are you talking about?

DON: The review!

MARGIE: Is it in there? Just tell me if they mentioned my name.

MANNY: Wait! Give me a moment to look.

DON: Where's Rod?

MANNY: I let him sleep in. *(Flipping through the newspaper.)* It's not here.

JANET: No review?

MANNY: The critics in this city sometimes place their reviews the following week.

MARGIE: What?!

JANET: A week! That's right, I forgot about that… It's been so long since we've had one.

MARGIE: We have to wait a week! I'm leaving today. I can't wait a week.

MANNY: *(Sits and opens the paper.)* I think everyone should just relax. The show wasn't that bad.

MARGIE: Are you kidding me? We burnt the baby Jesus!

JANET: I'm sure they're going to think we were making a political statement!

MARGIE: I think you mean racial.

JANET: Jesus was white.

MARGIE: Says you. I saw a black baby being tossed around.

JANET: He started out white.

DON: That's a social statement!

JIM: A baby Jesus burning, sounds more like a religious statement.

MANNY: People! It was an accidental fire, that's all, no *statement* was being made.

MARGIE: You know that, I know that, but the right wing religious conservatives don't know that.

JANET: And the critics!

JIM: Who were they Manny?

MANNY: Frontier Magazine. And this paper, the L.A. Times. *(Suddenly notices the review.)* Oh my God!

MARGIE: What?

JANET: What is it Manny?

MANNY: It's here!

MARGIE: Oh Lord, no!

DON: What does it say?

MANNY: *(Reading the headline.)* Santa takes dump in manger. *(They all sit as Manny continues to read.)*

MANNY: The gay playwright that gave us such forgettable productions as "Okla-Homo" and "The Wizard Is Odd" premiers his new work, "The Gayest Christmas Pageant Ever," at the Triangle Theater in West Hollywood last evening, and even a reputable New York director couldn't save this production. Why she chose this particular play to direct is beyond anyone's understanding. *(Margie moans.)* All this critic can possibly surmise is, she must have owed someone a favor.

MARGIE: I'm ruined.

MANNY: *(Continues.)* A novelty defecating Santa was the only redeemable part of this entire production.

DON: Shit.

MANNY: *(Continues.)* This adorable little plastic novelty actually spoke volumes about the play by eliminating on the actors and the set. A true case of art imitating life!

JANET: We're ruined.

MANNY: *(Continues.)* Filled with awful, over dramatic performances, one actor even moved his lips as others spoke. I haven't seen that since Middle School. A terrible set design *(Jim moans.)* making it possible to denigrate a stable. Let's not even discuss the grand finale of this horrendous production. Would you believe the burning of the baby Jesus? I know! Save your money, by a loved one a nice Christmas gift, or better yet, visit another theater presenting a true joy-filled Christmas production. This show is a mustn't see. *(Everyone sits in silence. Rod's voice is heard off stage.)*

ROD: Where is everybody?

MANNY: It's his fault. He moved the Shitting Santa.

DON: Here it comes. *(Rod enters with a smile on his face.)*

ROD: Hello.

MANNY: Hello?

ROD: Good morning!

MANNY: Good morning?

DON: You see the review?

ROD: Yes I did!

DON: And?

ROD: And?

DON: You're not upset?

ROD: Upset?

MANNY: What's up Rod?

ROD: *(Pauses, then very excited.)* We're sold out!

DON: What?

ROD: Yes!

MANNY: Sold out?

ROD: After the review came out the phones started ringing off the hook! Everyone wants to see the show! Thank you Jesus!

JESUS: *(Voiceover that only Jim can hear.)* It's Jesús. *(Spoken to emphasize the Spanish, pronounced "hay-SOO-oos." The voiceover is accented by a quick "special" on Jim.)*

JIM: *(Reacting to Jesus' voice.)* Holy crap! Did you hear that?

JANET: *(Referring to being sold out.)* Yes, it's great!

DON: Unbelievable.

MANNY: What a miracle.

JIM: *(Referring to Jesus.)* You heard it?

JANET: Of course we heard it Jim!

DON: What, you think we're deaf?

JIM: Oh my God, this is so cool! I thought I was the only one who could hear Jesús.

DON: Who?

JIM: Jesús.

DON: What?

MARGIE: (loudly breaking the moment) Great! Everyone in L.A. is coming to see a shit play with my name under director. I need to catch my flight.

ROD: How rude. *(Margie picks up her luggage and starts to exit.)*

MARGIE: Rod, I'm very happy for you. You finally have a hit show. I'm ruined. This has been quite an experience. Jim, thanks. Don, thank you for the check. Janet, if you're ever in the city call me. Manny, next time you need a director, FUCK OFF! *(Margie exits.)*

MANNY: Try to do someone a favor...

ROD: Who cares, we have a hit. We're are set for every Christmas from now on...

DON: *(to Manny)* You didn't tell him?

ROD: Tell me what?

DON: Someone has submitted another Christmas script for next year's pageant.

ROD: *(without hesitating)* I QUIT! *(exits)*

(Manny and Don talk as they exit)

MANNY: You couldn't fucking wait?

DON: Till when?

MANNY: Next year!

(they're gone)

JANET: Well, all's well that ends well. *(Janet starts to leave.)*

JIM: Hey.

JANET: Yes? *(Jim gives Don a look, Don exits.)*

JIM: Well?

JANET: What?

JIM: What about our dinner date?

JANET: Jim, I'm going to be honest with you...

JIM: You're not interested?

JANET: Jim, I don't think I can date someone who smokes pot and sees Jesus all the time.

JIM: I don't see Jesus *all* the time.

JANET: And the marijuana?

JIM: That's… *(Jesus enters and stands behind Janet.)* Oh no.

JANET: What is it?

JIM: If I told you I don't think you'd believe me.

JANET: Jim, what is it!

JIM: Jesus is standing behind you.

JANET: Oh for crying out loud Jim, are you stoned?

JIM: No! And that's what surprises me.

JANET: That you're not stoned?

JIM: That I see Jesus when I'm not stoned. *(Jesus pushes Janet into Jim's arms and they kiss.)*

JANET: *(Breaking out of the kiss.)* Jesus Christ.

JESUS: What? *(Janet turns, sees Jesus and screams. Jesus screams with her. They both stop.)*

JANET: Who the hell are you?

JESUS: Jesús.

JANET: You mean Jesus?

JESUS: Oh, dios mio.

JANET: If you're Jesus then I'm the Virgin Mary.

JESUS: Virgin? I don't think so. *(Snap. Janet grabs Jesus' beard and tries to pull it off as he gasps in pain.)*

JANET: It's real?

JESUS: Yes!

JANET: You grew a beard?

JESUS: Over two thousand years ago.

JANET: *(To Jim.)* This guy is good.

JIM: Janet, it's Jesús. *(Introducing them.)* Jesús, Janet.

JESUS: I know.

JANET: Who are you really?

JESUS: You don't believe your own eyes.

JANET: You're…

JESUS: The great "I am."

JANET: Prove it!

Jesus waves his arms and a loud clap of thunder is heard. Jesus snaps, a quick black out, and lights snap back up. Jesus is gone, and Janet is now a handsome man dressed in Janet's clothes with his back to the audience.

JANET: *(Just offstage.)* Jim?

JIM: Yeah?

HANDSOME MAN: *(Turns around, very surprised.)* I'm a guy!

JIM: *(Stunned and slowly interested.)* Yeah. *(Taking it in for a moment.)*

HANDSOME MAN: And I'm fucking hot!

JIM: Yeah, dude, you rock. *(Progressively it shows in their faces that they are attracted to each other.)*

HANDSOME MAN: You want some of this?

JIM: Sure do.

HANDSOME MAN: Let's hit it. *(As they walk off hand and hand, Jim addresses the audience.)*

JIM: I know what you are all thinking, but I've always been sexually fluid and now she'll definitely recieve equal pay!

SNAP TO BLACKOUT.

END OF SCENE 5.

ACT 2
SCENE 6

Back on the sidewalk in front of The Triangle Theatre Company. Only one male protester wearing a MAGA hat holding a "TRUMP 2020" sign is remaining. The female reporter is now sitting on the ground, Manny is holding the FOX News microphone for Rod.

ROD: Yes, all true… And that's our story. How a small LGBT community theatre in West Hollywood sold out every performance. And was host to Jesus Christ.
FEMALE REPORTER: *(standing and interrupting.)* Are you finished?
ROD: Not quite.
(Manny hands her the microphone as Rod walks to the protester)
FEMALE REPORTER: *(to Rod)* We've been off the air for two hours! *(a voice in her earbud)* What? Oh, *(composed)* and we're back live here in West Hollywood outside the Triangle Theatre Company. *(Rod grabs the "Trump 2020" sign and begins to attack the protester with it. The protester runs off stage followed by Rod. Manny and the reporter watch the action taking place just off stage, as the Female Reporter describes what's happening.)*
FEMALE REPORTER: Wait...one moment Tucker. It looks as if there's some comotion… no… it's… it's an attack… yes, the playwright slash director is attacking the Trump supporter. Yes, that's exactly what's happening… wait… he's taking the MAGA hat off the protester… he's stomping on it… he's shoving it down the back of his own pants and… oh that's disgusting… the protester is fighting mad… they're exchanging punches… the playwrights been, hit he's fallen to the ground, is this it? No… no, he's up again… Oh, he's mad, and *(a very loud slap is heard off)* now that's what you'd call a bitch slap and the Trump supporter has fallen to the ground. The playwright has not stopped his attack… he's hitting the protester with the Trump 2020 sign… the protester is slowly getting up to his feet… *(another loud slap off)* and it's another bitch slap to the supporter… *(another slap)* oh my that landed directly on target… and the protester is down… he's out cold… oh my, now what's happening? The playwright seems to be… is this really happening? Yes, yes, he's removed the Trump supporters pants… he's… he's… rolled up the Trump sign and he seems to be… oh no… he's not going to…
MANNY: It sure looks like it.
(A loud scream from the Trump Protester)
FEMALE REPORTER: Oh no...NO... the inhumanity! Tucker I can't, I can't describe the…
MANNY: I can! *(takes microphone looks out to audience)* It's safe again to say Happy Holidays...so Happy fucking Holidays FOX viewers!

SNAP TO BLACKOUT.

THE END.

PROP LIST

Act 1 Scene 1
- Cups of coffee
- Clipboard for Janet
- Microphone
- Signs for reporter
- Large Hat
- Sun Glasses
- Gay Slang Handbook
- 2 Shopping bags filled with props and gifts
- Pooping Santa Christmas tree topper
- Bolts of Fabric
- 2 manuscripts
- Lighter
- Mop

Act 1 Scene 2
- Script
- Walker
- Bag of chips

Act 1 Scene 3
- Joint

Act 1 Scene 4
- Headshots/resume
- Cup of coffee
- Satchel filled with sheet music, pens, paper, box of tissues, mints, fly swatter
- Keyboard
- Script for Margie
- Clipboard
- Large Pizza Box
- Cup of coffee

Act 1 Scene 5
- Costumes for Tarquin
- Pizza box for Alex
- Resume/Headshot for Jim
- 2 Guns
- Cup Of coffee

Act 2 Scene 1
- Hay
- Large Star
- Plastic Animals
- Cell phone
- Hammer
- 3 cans of soda
- Notebook
- Narrators Book
- Plastic Donkey

Act 2 Scene 2
- Trash Cans
- Joint
- Oranges
- Bong
- Martini Glasses
- Large Purse
- Dead Cat
- Gun
- Bucket with hole
- Clipboard for janet

Act 2 Scene 4
- Large Christmas Tree
- Keyboard
- Pooping Santa
- Baby Jesus White and Black
- Scroll
- Gold bling "Jesus" chain
- Air freshener
- Polo Black
- Cell Phones

Act 2 Scene 5
- Suitcase
- LA Times

Act 2 Scene 6
- God hates Flags sign
- Microphone

CPSIA information can be obtained
at www.ICGtesting.com
Printed in the USA
BVHW012153280621
610707BV00012B/312